MY
BILLIONAIRE
Fling

Maci Dillon

My Billionaire Fling
British Billionaires Book Two

Maci Dillon

This book is a work of fiction. Any references to real events, real people, and real places are used fictitiously. Other names, characters, places, and incidents are products of the author's imagination, and any resemblance to persons, living or dead, actual events, organizations, or places is entirely coincidental.

All rights are reserved. This book is intended for the purchaser of this e-book ONLY. No part of this book may be reproduced or transmitted in any form or by any means, graphic, electronic, or mechanical, including photocopying, recording, taping, or by any information storage retrieval system, without the express written permission of the author. All songs, song titles, and lyrics contained in this book are the property of the respective songwriters and copyright holders.

All efforts have been made to ensure the use of correct grammar and punctuation in the book. If you find any errors, please email Maci Dillon at admin@macidillonauthor.com Thank you.

ISBN: 979-8480472301

Editing by Swish Design & Editing
Proofreading by Swish Design & Editing
Book Design by Swish Design & Editing
Cover Design by Opium House Creatives
Cover Image Copyright 2021
First Edition 2021
Copyright © 2021 Maci Dillon
All Rights Reserved

DEDICATION

Ellen (Ellie), this one's for you.
Thank you for naming Sophia's first love, Incontro.

GLOSSAR

This series is set in London, UK and written in American English. You will find some British slang used in dialogue which you may not have heard before, so I have listed a few below.

Blimey - used to express surprise at something
Bonkers - mad, crazy
Cock-up - mistake, failure
Digs - housing, home
Dog's Bollocks - admirable, good at something
Gobby - used to describe someone who talks a lot
Jiffy - to do something immediately
Knackered - extremely tired, exhausted
Plastered - drunk, intoxicated
Plonker - foolish person
Nosh - food
Shambles - mess, confusion

Taking the mickey - to tease or make jokes

Tanked - drunk, intoxicated

MY BILLIONAIRE
Fling

PROLOGUE

SOPHIA
A Year Ago - June

"Brilliant speech, Miss Evans."

My voice fades mid-sentence while discussing the event with my assistant, Kelli, when I hear his velvety voice behind me. Turning, my gaze meets a set of simmering chocolate eyes and a sexy grin I pretend not to notice.

"Thank you, and you are?"

"Lugreno. Gabe Lugreno." He offers me his hand, and I take it with a smile.

"Well, Mr. Lugreno, what brings you to the gala tonight?"

The name sounds familiar, as if I should know who this man is. But I can't place him or where I might know him. And believe me, he's not a man who'd be easily forgotten.

1

"Please, call me Gabe. I'm too young to be a mister outside of the office."

Dressed to impress in a tux, I can't shake the vibe surrounding this impromptu encounter.

"I'm in town on business, and when I heard what you've been doing for child slavery, I had to come and check it out for myself."

He slides his hand inside his jacket, produces a white envelope, and passes it to me. "Consider this my contribution."

"Much appreciated. I assume the check is written out to the foundation?"

"Of course. Your parents would be very proud, Sophia."

The mention of my parents sends my stomach plummeting. Who is this man, and what would he know about my parents? A cold chill travels the length of my spine, and I suppress a shudder.

"Babe, there you are. I've been looking everywhere for you."

Before I have a chance to ask how he knows of my parents, a tall brunette with a painted-on gown brushes herself against the mystery man who has my senses on high alert.

And not in a good way.

Mostly.

Recognizing the woman as one of my clients at Incontro, my elite dating service, I offer a polite smile. "Hi, I'm Sophia Evans. Thank you for joining us tonight."

She returns my smile, and I see the relief in her eyes as I pretend not to recognize her. Many of my clients support this event annually, knowing what it means to me. And I'd never out one of my clients.

"It's a wonderful evening, as always. I'm Marnie," the woman offers before turning to Mr. Lugreno. "We should dance."

Gabe concedes and follows her to the dance floor, throwing me a casually wicked glance over his shoulder.

What a player.

An hour after the last guests have left, Kelli and I are about to head out when one of the event staff approach me uncomfortably. "Ah, Miss Evans, I've been asked to pass this along to you with regards from Mr. Lugreno."

Hesitantly, I accept the note and slip it inside my purse, ignoring Kelli's questioning glance.

Chapter 1

SOPHIA

"Kelli, can I see you for a moment, please?" I breeze through the front doors of Incontro past the front desk, where Kelli has worked diligently by my side since the beginning.

"Of course, I'll be right there," she answers, pushing back from her computer and rushes to the kitchenette.

As I enter my office later than usual for a Monday morning, I fall into my chair and open my laptop. My office is light and airy where a few intimate portraits painted by my brother, Jarett, line the walls with quotes about love and relationships. The desk where I spend most of my days when not with clients is spotless and free of clutter. Exactly how I left it on Saturday.

Did I mention I'm married to my work?

Recently passing the thirty-nine-year mark, I've spent most of my adult life learning about the human psyche, evaluating personal relationships, core values, and matching potential suitors, coaching clients through the perfect dates, and working one on one guiding clients through their romantic beliefs and expectations.

Loving what I do and despite the constant ridicule of being a single woman devoted to the happiness of others, I wouldn't change my profession for the world. Nothing makes me happier than matching two people together who may never have had the chance without our services.

Kelli enters shortly after with a latte for each of us.

"Big night at Maximum, boss?" She chuckles, knowing I'm prone to be sluggish on a Monday after our weekly catch-up at Maxine's speakeasy.

"Ugh, big weekend in general." Kelli nods. Having stayed until the very end of the gala, she can appreciate how exhausting it is to work until three in the morning on Sunday and show up at the office again the following day.

"Mmm, best coffee ever," I drawl as I relax into my padded chair, cross my legs, and consider what I need from Kelli today.

She waits patiently, notebook in hand, pen at the ready.

"Does the name, Lugreno, mean anything to you?"

Fine lines crease her forehead at my question.

"As in the guy you met at the gala?"

Of course, she'd been with me when he approached and didn't appear to know who he was. "Want me to look into him?"

"Discreetly, yes. Report back to me before lunch with anything you find." She nods, narrowing her eyes at me.

"May I ask, as your friend, not your assistant, is this for personal or business purposes?"

Kelli has been my assistant for seven years. When I launched Incontro, she weighed in on the location of our office we secured in downtown Central London after months of searching for the right place to call home. We first met at college. Two years younger than me, she was studying business with psychology as her second major while I slogged away at my master's in human psychology.

"As you well know, everything I do is related to this business. It's my life."

The answer satisfies her, though I don't miss the cheeky side grin as she opens the door of my office, ready to leave.

"Please also check the last few matches and meetings for a client named Marnie Callaghan, would you?"

"Consider it done."

Pulling a small, folded note from my bag, I open it and lay it flat on my mouse pad.

> *Lunch Monday at noon.*
> *Maryland's Bar & Grill.*
> *Gabe L.*

Unsure what to think of this mysterious invitation and why he wants to meet with me, I pop it into my bottom drawer and try to focus on the events of the day. I have meetings with potential new clients after a boardroom meeting with my consultants in twenty minutes.

On returning to my office at the end of the morning, I check the time until my elusive lunch with Mr. Lugreno.

"You have a lunch meeting on your calendar. Do you have a moment to discuss my findings before you leave?" Kelli stands in the doorway of my office as I finish up a prerequisite meeting with a new client on the phone.

Without glancing up, I signal for her to come in and take a seat.

"What did you find?"

"Nada."

I'm surprised to hear she has shown up without a single piece of information. She places a client report in front of me. A quick perusal for the name, Gabe Lugreno, shows Marnie wasn't in attendance

7

with him due to any association with this agency.

"He's never been a client?" I shift my focus to Kelli, who's rocking back and forth on her heels, arms crossed, a knowing smile on her lips.

"He's your lunch appointment, isn't he?"

Nothing gets past Kelli.

Ever.

"Business meeting, yes."

"Ah-ha." She gleams teasingly. As I roll my eyes at her, she adds, "Never been a client. You may know his name from Lugreno Enterprises, though. Perhaps Jarett has had something to do with them on one of his properties."

Possibly. Jarett dabbles in property investment as if his crazy artistic talents and owning a well-sought-after gallery isn't enough to manage.

"If you don't intend to sleep with him, what does it matter if he's been a client or not?" Kelli doesn't dance around a situation but surges head-on into the depths of it, no fucks given. Usually, it's one of the many things I love about her.

Usually.

Shuffling papers on my desk, I prepare for my absence over lunch, knowing if I pay attention to her incessant need for gossip, I'll never hear the end of it.

"It matters because I have no idea why he's called a meeting."

And, because she's not far off base. While

younger than me and not my normal type, the man holds a part of my womanhood for ransom. An itch I can usually scratch myself shows no sign of dissipating.

He's been on my mind all weekend.

Aware of my hormonal inclination toward the stranger, I shield myself with a thicker-than-usual wall before I walk into the restaurant and lock eyes with him. No way in hell will he ever know he makes me weak in his presence.

As I stride across the busy dining room in his direction, he stands to greet me. "Sophia, thank you for meeting me on such short notice." He offers his hand as expected at a business luncheon.

The heated kiss he places on the back of my hand, *not so much.*

Torn between flattered and disheveled, I mentally adjust my armor and slide gracefully into the chair opposite him.

"I trust you won't mind I ordered for us both?" He grins as the waiter appears with a flaming grill plate with a huge serving of sticky ribs and nothing resembling a salad.

Yes, I mind.

He places the pile of meat-covered animal skeletons between us while a young waitress rushes to his side with a plate for each of us.

As a woman with good business sense, I smile politely and kindly ask the waiter for a Caesar salad to accompany the side of slaughtered pig.

Gabe laughs hard at my request, catching me off-guard. "Didn't pick you for the type to be scared of getting messy over a meal."

"You picked that up in the thirty seconds we spoke at the gala?"

He shakes his head. "No, but I was quick to note you're a woman who loves a challenge. Hence, why in the middle of your workday, you're about to eat a meal with a stranger... with your hands."

Throwing my head back, I laugh at his assessment.

Ten points for meeting me head-on with a challenge. One I'll never back down from.

My gaze narrows on his whimsical expression as my laughter fades to silence.

"What am I doing here, and how do you know of my parents?"

Now it's his turn to appear floored.

While waiting patiently for a response, my gaze follows the sauce from the rib he's slowly devouring as it smears his cheek. His eyes are steadfast and focused on me, but I continue to stare without concern.

Licking his fingers, one by one, I clench my thighs tightly beneath the table.

The fucker knows exactly what he's doing to me, but I want answers.

"There's a thing called Google. You'd be amazed

at the information provided online. You should check it out, but I imagine you searched my name before meeting with me today."

I may have, but that's beside the point.

Annoyed at his deflection, I press a little harder. "You searched for information on my parents?"

"Of course not, I searched for information on you, and I happened upon an article or two."

He searches my eyes until my gaze falls to the plate of food between us. Picking up a messy rib to fill the silence—due to my lack of response—I moan at the saucy deliciousness.

A smile threatens the corner of his mouth, and his eyes darken as he watches my mouth with anticipation.

Yeah, two can play this game.

"Does it bother you that I mentioned your parents?" he finally speaks.

"It bothers me that you googled me in the first place," I respond, wiping my hands clean.

"A friend of mine in New York has a cousin with an adult matchmaking service, similar to yours but more for the common folk rather than the elite."

Finally, we get to the reason for this meeting. Let's get it over with so I can get on with my day. "Go on," I encourage him, thanking the waiter as he returns with my salad and pours each of us a glass of wine.

"Due to family circumstances, they're looking to

sell. Perhaps you'd be interested in taking over and branching out internationally?"

"What makes you think I'd be interested in expanding?"

"You're a go-getter, and you have the money to support a move like that."

The fuck?

"You have no idea of my financial situation, Mr. Lugreno, nor is this something I wish to discuss with a man I don't know or trust." Astounded at the nerve of his comments, I gulp down my wine to wash away the growing agitation.

"I know enough. Your parents left a substantial fortune when they died, split between you and your siblings."

"If you'd done your research correctly, you'd know they didn't *die*, they were *killed*." The words taste like charred donkey as they fall from my mouth.

"In a plane crash, I know."

Emotions bubble up, and I struggle to contain them.

"It was no accident, as I'm sure you're aware." Tossing my salad around the plate, my appetite fades, along with my desire to continue this discussion. "If you'd like to send through some details on the sale of the business, please feel free." Pushing the plate aside, I pull a business card from my purse. Handing it across the table, I add, "If there's nothing else, I must be getting back to the office."

Gabe nods solemnly, accepting the card. "Of course. Can we see each other again?"

Amazed at his brazenness, I quip, "I imagine if I want more information, I'll speak directly to the owner."

"Business aside. Let's do dinner tomorrow night before I fly back to the states."

I consider his date with Marnie only two days ago.

"Marnie, was it? We met at the gala."

"A date with an acquaintance. You, of all people, know all dates aren't created equal."

Unprepared to give him an answer while not thinking clearly, I smile. "Send me the details of the potential business opportunity, and I'll get back to you."

Chapter
2

SOPHIA

"Jarett, hi."

"You sound knackered, sis. What's the problem?"

"Since when do I need an excuse for calling my baby bro?"

Jarett laughs, something I don't hear as often as I like anymore. Since the tragic death of his wife, Helena, he has lost his way somewhat.

"Never, I'm taking the mickey."

"I'm about to leave the city and head home. Are you free to meet me? I have a business proposal I'd love you to look over for me."

"Sure, drop in. I'm at the gallery. But ah, isn't this something you should be taking to Roman?"

Roman is our older brother and has been in business the longest. Plus, he completed his Master's in Business and Economics long before becoming a chef and opening his café.

"Already have. I want a second opinion."

Technically, his will be the third set of eyes going over it since I ran it by Kelli this afternoon. After all, she'll need to be onboard if we decide to move on this opportunity. Inevitably, it will land in the hands of our legal team before any decision is made, but Jarett is and always has been my biggest supporter.

"Ouch, the rebound opinion."

Chuckling into the phone, I set the security alarm and exit the building. "I prefer to see it as leaving the best 'til last."

"Ah, you've earned it. See you soon."

It's not that I haven't thought of taking the business international before, but the opportunity has never presented itself like this. Nor have I gone out of my way to uncover one. The least I can do is give this solid consideration.

My phone pings with a message as I stroll through the streets toward Jarett's art gallery. He spends more time there than at home since the accident, and as much as I try not to mention it, I worry about him.

Tapping on the unknown number, my steps slow in pace as I read the message.

Unknown: *Still waiting on your answer. And I don't mean the business proposal.*

Ugh. I'm about to lose my shit and blast him with a how-the-fuck did you get my number when I remember I gave him my business card. That was a poorly guarded decision.

Choosing to ignore the message for now, I keep my focus on the business at hand.

After an hour with Jarett, I'm comfortable with the idea of approaching my legal team about a potential offer of the New York agency. The clientele is considerably different, but their membership base is quite substantial. Adding the Incontro branding and introducing an elite membership option in line with what we offer our Londoner's will create a positive enhancement and be a feeding ground for growth.

It's close to nine in the evening before I walk into my apartment in Shoreditch. I'm grateful for the Uber Eats delivery Jarett organized for us. I place my briefcase on the countertop in the kitchen, kick off my heels, eagerly unclasp my bra, and pull it from beneath my dress.

Ahh, letting the girls out and padding barefoot around my home after a big day is the best feeling in the world. Considering a bubble bath to relax with a glass of wine, I settle on just cabernet instead. My eyes are too heavy to soak in the tub. I'd never want to get out.

Activating Alexa, I request my evening mood playlist and relax on the sofa, my feet propped up on the footstool in front of me. I lay my head back and listen to "Afterglow" by Ed Sheeran fill the room, the melody of his voice transporting me to a happy place.

Until my phone breaks the mood and beckons my attention.

> **Unknown:** *Dinner at seven? Cutlery included.*

Chuckling, I add his number to my contacts list and tap out a reply.

> **Me:** *I'd like to talk more about the business opportunity.*

Dots dance across the screen as he types a response.

> **Gabe:** *Call me tomorrow. I don't talk business on dates.*

I smile. Dating rule one-o-one, never discuss business or work on a first date. Except this isn't a date.

> **Me:** *Lucky this isn't a date.*

My phone buzzes with an incoming call, his

name scrolling across the screen. I consider letting it go to voicemail, but instead, I do the adult thing and swipe to answer. Before I have a chance to greet him, his voice booms through my cell.

"A date is exactly what this is, Sophia. I'll pick you up from Incontro at seven o'clock."

"Are you always this bossy?" I snap, pretending to be annoyed.

"You have no idea."

"Ah, Gabe." My voice delivers the words in a breathy moan, unable to stop visualizing just how bossy he'd be in bed. "Dinner and nothing more."

"That sounds like a challenge I'm up for. Good night, Sophia."

The call ends, leaving me riled up and the opposite of how I felt when I walked in a short time ago. Taking my laptop from my bag, I pour another glass of wine and settle in to do some research of my own. *Who is Mr. Lugreno?* I fire up Google and type in Gabe Lugreno.

Most of what I find relates to Lugreno Enterprises with the odd image of him with multiple women at his side at social events in New York City. He doesn't appear to be the center of any scandals or newsworthy social drama which is a bonus.

Apart from a young, successful CEO with billions to his name, he appears to be a mediocre human on the verge of boring. I can't even find any personal social media accounts.

The way he looks at me, it's hard to believe the man could be boring at anything. Clearly, he's well versed in keeping his private life, private—a value I respect and one we have in common.

Satisfied I haven't agreed to a *date* with a self-absorbed, entitled socialite with a personal agenda outside of getting laid, I close my laptop and retreat to my bedroom to prepare for a much-needed, long hot shower.

Chapter 3

SOPHIA

Midday Tuesday, I have a few hours to spare between appointments. With my mind wandering through unchartered territory about tonight's dinner invitation with the perplexing Mr. Lugreno, I find myself at my favorite vintage store pushing back items on the rack in search of who knows what.

In need of some perspective, I ask Holly to meet me last minute. As always, my childhood friend since the age of five comes running to my aid, loaded with every type of response she thinks I might need.

"I knew this was about a man the second you called."

"It's not about *a* man. It's about *Gabe*... he's different."

Holly laughs, pulling a hideous off-green sixties dress from the back of a nearby rack and holding it up against her.

"What's so special about this one?"

"The dress?" I joke.

"The man," she clarifies, rolling her eyes at me.

Frustration pours out of me with a string of words I don't understand until they're out in the open. "I never said special. Different, as in, I think I want to go on a date with him, and we both know I don't date. Fuck, Holly, I only entertain a man if I really have an itch to scratch. I'm almost forty with no interest in a relationship, casual dating included. Yet, here I am, considering a date with a younger, successful man who commands my attention with a single look and softens my need for control in a dangerous way."

Holly stares back at me as I take a deep breath, her eyes wide. My admission comes as a shock to both of us. For once, I let the words flow without inhibition. I've trained myself to only divulge certain pieces of information which pertain to my personal life, as this is required in my line of work. And quite simply, most of my waking moments involve work with or for my clients.

"Holy shit, lady. Who is this guy who's got you so twisted up?"

"I mean, he's American, arrogant, and incapable of taking no for an answer, but he doesn't live here, so—"

"Exactly! Date the guy, fuck his brains out, and give in to your need for control for once. Let him own your body for a good few hours and wave goodbye forever once he's back on that plane."

"Jet."

"Excuse me?"

"I doubt he travels internationally on a passenger flight. My guess is, as the CEO of a multi-billion-dollar company, he has a jet."

Holly pouts sarcastically at this news and swats my shoulder.

"Do it already. Say yes to the date and forget all about him. Loaded or not, let's assume he's young and dumb and needs a woman like you to remind him he's not all that."

Now it's my turn to laugh.

I'm certain he knows he's all that and more. As for young and dumb—I bet my monthly turnover that he's used those eyes to pull more women into bed than I've had lattes—his strong forearms and perfectly crafted hands suggest he's a man of many pleasures in bed.

I'm so screwed.

Yet, ten minutes before seven, I give myself a quick once-over in my office's private bathroom. Giving the girls a squeeze, I ensure they're plastered in place beneath the low-cut fifties swing dress I have cinched at the waist with a wide belt and finished off with a pair of strappy stilettos.

Scrunching my thick brown locks, I give the few curls I added with my portable curling wand an extra boost. With an extra coat of blood-red lipstick, I smack my lips together loudly. I'm asking for trouble looking this damn hot for a date with the devilish Mr. Lugreno.

Clutch in hand, I turn off the light on the way out of my office. As I'm setting the alarm and locking the main door, a town car arrives on the street behind me. Turning, I swoon at the sight of Gabe as he exits the back seat in a dress shirt rolled to the elbows and dress pants filled to perfection in all the right places.

His eyes narrow in on my face, heated and needy as they descend the length of my dress and return to my cleavage. Exactly the reaction I expected.

"Right on time, Mr. Lugreno."

"You look incredible," he answers, a hungry grin crossing his face.

To steady me as I make my way inside the vehicle, he offers his hand and I'm all too aware of the sizzling heat in his touch. With a single inhale, I already know his masculine scent will be hard to forget. "Hello, Miss Evans," his driver greets me politely.

"Meet Viktor, my driver while in London."

"Lovely to meet you, Viktor. Whatever did you do to deserve Mr. Lugreno as your boss?" I joke.

Gabe smirks as he buckles up.

"Mr. Lugreno is the best boss an old man like me could ask for." Viktor laughs, winking at me over his shoulder before he turns his attention to the road and driving us to our dinner destination.

"You have five minutes until we get to the restaurant. Now is your only chance to talk business." Gabe glances at me, waiting patiently.

"Fine. I've looked over the details with a few confidants and sent it through to my legal team for review. At first glance, it appears to be an opportunity I'm happy to pursue further."

Gabe nods. "I thought it might be a perfect fit, although a slightly different clientele to what you have here."

"Yes, I believe we can expand and diversify the clientele with time. Do you mind me asking why your friend's cousin is wanting to sell?"

"Medical expenses are piling up for Bree's parents, and all responsibility falls back on her. The sale of her business is the only opportunity available to her to satisfy them. Sadly, it's not her first choice but the only one."

My heart twists for the agony she must be experiencing with such a decision, if having sick parents wouldn't be enough stress. "Would she consider staying on to run the agency after the sale? Tremendously compensated for her efforts, of course."

Gabe's expression softens after a brief look of surprise. "Is that something you would consider?"

"Of course, I'd want to meet with Bree and get a feel for her as a person and a business partner, but if it could be helpful for both of us, why not? Taking over an established company of any form, replacing employees isn't my preferred choice. I'd rather work with those who are already committed to the success of the business."

A small smile lingers as he contemplates my answer. "I'm sure Bree would be happy to hear this. When do you think you could get out to New York?"

"As soon as possible, preferably. End of next week? Thursday and Friday perhaps, for an in-office tour and to meet the staff on a casual basis. I could do with a weekend away, so I'll arrange to stay until Monday. It won't take much to reschedule my responsibilities here, and my team is more than capable in my absence for a few days."

"We're approaching now, sir," Viktor calls from the front, and Gabe acknowledges with a slight nod in his direction.

"Consider it done. Book your flights and send me the details."

Glancing out the window, I notice we're pulling up to the city's most honorable French dining experience. Not only does it have three Michelin stars but also houses the most famous dining table in London.

I've never had the pleasure of experiencing it personally, but I've heard the table is situated in the middle of the dining room, and shimmering lights fall around it, creating an opulent and private dining experience.

"Wow, you sure do pull out all the stops, don't you?"

"What's the point of making bank and not enjoying an expensive meal out with a beautiful woman?"

While I choose not to live the billionaire lifestyle with drivers and private jets at the ready, I can't argue with his logic in the slightest.

He takes my hand when the car hums to a stop in the valet entrance, and Viktor rushes to open the door. Gabe sends him off with the promise to call when we're finished with the evening.

Chapter 4

SOPHIA

A young French waiter shows us to our table toward the back of the dining room.

Once seated, Gabe orders a bottle of wine to share, and I happily take him up on his offer to order my meal this evening.

"How often do you fly to London for business?"

"As often as required, depends on the projects I'm working on."

"You don't have a permanent office here?"

Gabe shakes his head. "No. If necessary, I hire a space for the length of time to conclude the existing project, but the suite I stay in is well-equipped with a large office. I conduct most of my work from there, but for the most part, I'm hands on with my clients."

I do like a hands-on man.

When a senior waiter arrives to introduce himself and take our order, I take a minute to peruse the menu. Gabe knows exactly what he wants, clearly familiar with the offerings. No doubt he brings all his dates here to lure them into bed.

When we're alone again, Gabe continues, "My assistant, Elise, sometimes travels with me, and when that happens, I rent a space she can work from or at least make sure her hotel has ample office space. I don't allow just *any* woman into my room."

"Oh," I quip. "So you're a ladies' man with standards?"

"You wouldn't be here if I weren't. A ladies' man, that is." His grin spreads like wildfire across his face, and it's hard not to smile in return.

"Why are we talking about work, anyway? I told you the rule. No business talk on a date."

"We aren't discussing business. I'm trying to get to know you."

"How about I ask the questions?"

"Fine, ask away."

Over dinner, we play a game of twenty questions, Gabe style. The conversation flows easily, and I'm surprised by the effortless banter between us.

The waiter returns to check on our meals. "Perfect, thank you," I assure him with a smile. I'm part way through my Alaskan king crab and green pepper curry. Gabe settled on the sea urchin with potato foam and creamy champagne sauce. The menu is exquisite, and the meals are extraordinary.

"Would you like a dessert menu to follow, sir?" the waiter addresses Gabe.

"Thank you, if you wouldn't mind," he answers, wiping the corner of his mouth with the linen napkin. A spot of sauce remains on the opposite side of his lips, and it takes all my willpower to remain in my seat and not reach forward to lick up the yummy goodness, stealing a taste of his perfectly kissable mouth at the same time.

An hour later, we're learning we have more in common than I imagined. As the wine keeps coming, it becomes blatantly clear saying no to this man is going to be one of the hardest things I ever have to do.

"Favorite city?" I ask.

"Hmm, I love Paris for the food and art, but strangely enough, I can't go past a weekend in Seattle. There's something about the ferry boats that intrigue me." I chuckle, happy to hear he's human, after all.

"Paris is by far my favorite. I haven't been to New York before, so I'm looking forward to next weekend."

"Never?"

"Uh-ha, never say never." I laugh. "Never is for people with no will to succeed."

He raises his glass to me, and we toast. "I love the way you think, Sophia."

No doubt he'd love a transcript of my current dirty thoughts.

"I'll have my assistant schedule in some sightseeing while you're in New York. You can't say you've been without photos at all the main attractions."

"Sounds like a plan. I've always wanted to see the Statue of Liberty. I believe you can go all the way up to the crown."

"It's usually booked well in advance for entry into the crown, but I'll try anything once."

No doubt you would.

"What's that smirk for?"

Busted. Damn my sinfully delicious thoughts.

"Who, me?" I joke, spinning around as if he must be speaking about somebody else. That's when I see most of the diners have left for the evening.

"Are you thinking what I'm thinking?" He grins when my focus returns to him.

Intrigued, I place my elbows on the table, link my hands together, and rest my chin in my knuckles. "You got me. What are we thinking?"

"It's getting late. And late nights with wine and good company lead to straight past the *dinner-only* gate."

"Oh, they do?" I feign ignorance and take another sip of fruity goodness. "I'm sadly unaware. It's not often I enter the *date* gate."

Amused, Gabe chuckles, the sound genuine and refreshing to my ears.

"I find that hard to believe, Sophia. You're a beautiful woman crowned with grace and success. All the single men of London must beg for your company."

Laughter bursts from my chest at the idea this man has about me.

"I'm afraid you're mistaken. Most men who are emotionally available are threatened by my success and power."

"As they should be. But I'm not *most* men."

No, you're the type of man I avoid at all costs.

"Gabe..." His name leaves my lips in a breathy gasp. Engaged in conversation all the way home after dinner, I gave no thought to where we might be going. Now the car has pulled to a stop, I peep through the window and see we've arrived at the Palace, where I suspect Gabe spends his nights while visiting the city on business.

"Join me for a night cap." He motions for me to step out of the car with him, and as much as I want to, he's now involved in my business dealings, and

I refuse to mix business with pleasure. Telling him so only gives cause for him to refute the feeble excuse.

"Bringing an opportunity to you isn't the same as going into business together. Believe me, there's nothing business-like about my attraction to you, Sophia." He brushes a curl back from my face, a simple touch that ignites flames even the London Fire Brigade would struggle to eliminate.

"What sort of nightcap are we talking about?" With the fruity sensation of our dinner wine still a velvety presence in my mouth, a gin and soda could sway my decision.

"With twenty-four-hour room service and access to an open bar, the choice is all yours, sweetheart."

Maybe it's the wine or my overactive sex drive, but sweetheart whispered in his American accent makes me gush in a way I'm thankful I wore panties. I extend my hand and allow him to guide me to his suite.

Inside the elevator, he keeps his eyes locked on the flashing lights as we ascend each floor. Unable to stand the tension building between us any longer, I press my palm into his shoulder, spinning him until he faces me and push him unapologetically against the wall.

His mouth falls open, and his eyes darken with lust. Like a wanton church-going woman unable to deny the sin of a man's touch, I crash my lips to his in a heated frenzy.

Before I know it, I'm grinding myself shamelessly over his thigh. His hand slips beneath the skirt of my dress, and he groans when his fingers meet the damp heat of my pussy through my thong. "Fuck, Sophia. You're so wet."

"Isn't this what you wanted?" I whisper breathlessly as he works his fingers over my clit.

"I want all of you in every way possible."

My hands are everywhere but not close enough. I pull his shirt from his pants and with frenzied fingers, attempt to flick open the buttons.

Oh, fuck it.

Buttons pop from the shirt and fall to the ground as I tear it open, exposing his toned chest. "Fuck me," he growls, inserting his finger into my fiery heat. A light smattering of hair covers his pecs, and I salivate at the rippling six-pack beneath my fingers, tensing with every movement as he finger-fucks me.

Almost at the point of no return, my lips caress his chest, and I lick my way up his neck when the elevator signals our arrival and the doors open. Gabe pushes me out and takes my hand, pulling me behind him until we're inside his room. He pins me against the wall with his chest and removes his jacket and buttonless shirt.

Quickly, he lifts my dress and grins wickedly, taking my thong in his fingers, and this time,

33

instead of pulling it to the side, he tears it from my body with ease. My head falls back completely at his mercy as he bends down, hooks his arms around my thighs, and lifts me. I shriek at the sudden movement.

"I got you, sweetheart."

Gabe is standing tall, my pussy open at his mouth and my back straight, pinned to the wall. I'm literally on top of the world at this moment.

Holding me in place, high above him, I thank the universe for high ceilings and men who can lift. My legs rest over his shoulders as he licks the length of my wetness, groaning like a starved man. Teasing me with the heat of his tongue and precision of his touch, he masterfully swirls his tongue around my clit, flicking the hardened nub until I see stars and writhe against him.

When I think I can't take it any longer, his tongue darts between my lips, lapping at my juices.

"Holy fuck, Gabe."

"Mmm," he moans against me, the hum on my pussy only pushing me further to the edge.

"I'm so close," I weep, clutching his hair tightly as I ride his face.

I've never been so desperate to come, yet so unwillingly to reach the end of an orgasm in my life.

"Give it to me, sweetheart. Come on my face."

It's all I need to succumb to the abyss which is Gabe fucking Lugreno.

Once my body stops convulsing with tortured pleasure, he lowers me to the floor and adjusts himself in his pants. "We better get you out of those pants and take care of that."

"I thought you'd never ask," he says, stripping naked.

When his cock springs free from its confines, I gulp, momentarily rethinking the situation. This guy is going to break me.

And I'm going to love every fucking minute of it.

"Oh, I didn't ask." Walking further into his suite, I'm unsure where he wants me.

His gaze challenges me as I shrug out of my dress and remove my bra and heels. My body burns from the inside out under his watchful eye, standing naked before him.

"Turn around." He stalks toward me as I turn away. "Over the sofa."

His words are clipped, and his voice is rough. Taking two steps to the sofa, I lean forward over the chair's arm, my ass facing him. Ready and waiting.

Behind me, I hear him tearing open a packet and sheathing himself with a condom.

To better support myself on my elbows, I stretch further forward. Gabe runs his cock through my folds and, without a single word, edges inside.

"Relax, sweetheart."

A pleasurable moan escapes me as he fills me, gliding in and out at a teasingly slow pace. "Ah,

35

fuck." As he massages the globes of my ass, he quickens the pace, flexing his strong hips, driving me deeper into the cushions. "This won't last long... your pussy is too fucking hot."

Between his accent and his dirty talk, I'm fast approaching my second release. "So... fucking good..." I moan, ignoring the chair's arm digging into me.

He slaps my ass and ramps up the power of his movements until my muffled groans turn to outright cries of pleasure when I convulse around his cock. He reaches his release with a gratifying grunt and rubs his hands over my back as we both calm down and catch our breath.

Before cleaning himself up and fetching us some drinks, he helps me to my feet, and directs me to the bathroom.

Chapter
5

SOPHIA
New York City - June

Gabe is waiting for me as I disembark and collect my luggage at JFK. Although I'm only staying four nights, I have ample outfits to see me through a month. Nobody will ever accuse me of packing light. I considered paying extra for a second suitcase of shoes, but I figured I'd have plenty of time to shop for new ones on my mini vay-cay.

We have a meeting with Bree at Heavenly Matches in two hours, and Gabe assures me I'll have plenty of time to check in at my hotel and freshen up.

"You made it." He grins, looking behind me at my oversized case, the wheels screeching at the strain of the weight. "I thought your return ticket was for Monday or was that Monday next month?"

"Don't get smart with me, Lugreno. Who knows what I might need over the next few days? I included something sexy for every occasion." I wink.

He holds his hands up, his expression serious. "Not arguing with sexy."

I flash him a sarcastic look as he takes my bag and leads the way to the car.

"I really didn't need you to collect me. I'm quite prepared to Uber into the city."

"My driver is on my payroll. He gets paid whether he's working or not, so you may as well utilize him during your stay. I'll send you his number, be sure to call him any time."

Not familiar with New York, I appreciate the offer, though it's completely unnecessary.

"Henry, this is Sophia Evans," Gabe introduces me to a frail older gentleman standing by the car with the door open and waiting. "I'll program her number into your phone. She's free to call you for any of her travel needs while she is visiting."

Henry nods in my direction, "Welcome to New York, Miss Evans."

"Thank you. Nice to meet you, Henry."

Mid-morning traffic into Manhattan is as bad as our peak hour back home. I'm grateful to have Henry at my beck and call if this is what I can expect. It's approximately forty-five minutes in this craziness to my hotel.

"I upgraded you to the suite at your hotel, no extra charge."

My head whips around at Gabe, almost forgetting he was sitting beside me as I take in the city streets. "Um, thank you. How di—"

His sharp glare cuts me off. He doesn't take kindly to questions of his ability to get shit done.

He's Gabe fucking Lugreno—people bend at his will.

Two hours into my meeting with Bree, I'm reluctant to finish up. She's an absolute gem of a woman, whose business sense and management skills rival my own. After meeting all of her consultant team, checking out the agency's internal workings, and going through the books with her, I'm convinced the purchase of Heavenly Matches is the perfect opportunity to take Incontro international.

"So, you would be willing to stay on in your current role at the agreed salary?"

Bree reaches across the table at the coffee shop, directly opposite her office, and squeezes my hand. "I'd be honored. I can't express how grateful I am for the opportunity."

I wave off her gratitude, "There's nobody more

suited for the position."

"There you two are." I turn at the sound of Gabe's voice. "I'm amazed you stopped talking long enough to eat," he adds, pointing at the dinner plates pushed to the corner of the table.

"What are you doing here? I thought I was meeting you for drinks at five?"

"Bree's cousin, Ben, will be meeting us at our usual cocktail bar. I thought I'd extend the invitation to Bree. Would you like to join us?"

Bree smiles sadly. "Thank you, but I'll have to pass. I'm going to the hospital tonight to visit with my father before his next surgery scheduled for tomorrow."

As strong as her exterior is, I feel her pain on a level I wish I never knew. "Of course. I hope everything goes well." I offer her a sympathetic smile, the kind I always hated to receive, but it's difficult not to sympathize.

Gabe nods. "Sure. I trust your meeting with Sophia has helped to lessen the burden for you."

A genuine smile crosses her face, and she clasps her hands together in excitement.

"Yes, it has. Thank you for setting this up. I believe my baby will be in the best hands with Sophia, and I'm looking forward to seeing where she takes us."

Ready to leave, I stand and secure my handbag over my arm. "I'll have my team prepare the documents and send them through to you early next week. Thank you for meeting with me and showing me around." Bending to hug Bree goodbye, I wish her all the best.

"Didn't mean to interrupt," Gabe says as we leave.

"No, I need to finish up, and I have some paperwork to address before we meet for drinks."

Ignoring me, he continues, "You'll love Ben, he's a straight shooter and a real ladies' man."

The jet, the suite upgrade, plans for drinks, meeting a friend, it all sounds a little too much like a couple's weekend trip away. Concerned about giving Gabe the wrong idea about us, I explain, "This isn't a date, you know. You and me," I say, pointing between us. "This is just business."

"Ahh, yes. And you're about to go into business with Ben's closest cousin, so think of it as meeting the new business family."

"Whatever you say." I smirk, unable to miss his cheeky side grin from the corner of my eye.

Chapter 6

SOPHIA

Jetlag is a bitch.

My paperwork ends in me falling asleep in a pile of mess on the bed.

I'm thankful to Henry for banging on my door after a few missed calls to wake me up. Gabe had him contact me a half-hour before leaving in case this exact thing happened. I failed to disable the silent mode on my phone after the meeting with Bree, and with no intention of falling asleep, didn't set the alarm.

A quick shower and rush job on my makeup leaves little time to style my hair, so I go with a messy-bun to complete my urban street look. My oversized sunglasses will help to mask the tell-tale signs of my afternoon nap.

I hope.

Henry appears to be impressed with my timing when I meet him downstairs. "Yes, sir," he speaks into his phone. "Miss Evans is on her way."

I roll my eyes at the idea of him checking up on me. I'm a grown-ass woman, and fuck, I'm older than he is. Only by six years, but in man-years, that's a lot of maturity.

Feeling very Carrie Bradshaw on her way to meet Mr. Big, I chuckle to myself. Why have I never been to New York before?

"Henry," I call from the back seat. "I'd love to do some shopping tomorrow. Will you be free to chauffer me?" I don't expect the old guy to accompany me from store to store, but I'll be needing somewhere to keep my purchases safe and manageable. And I'm going to need a new suitcase to fly it all home.

Excited about hitting the boutiques tomorrow, I'm oblivious that we're stationary, and Henry is waiting on me to get out. "Oh, my bad. Thank you so much." He silently nods as I step out onto the curb, and follow the direction of his gaze to find Gabe walking my way.

"Enjoy your nap?"

"Yes, I did. Thanks for asking," I grin and take his hand, allowing him to lead the way inside.

"What's your cocktail of choice?" he asks as we make our way to the bar. "A margarita, or pretty much anything that contains tequila." His top lip curls in a half-smirk, and his eyes linger on my face. "What?"

He shakes his head. "Nothing. I respect a woman who knows what she wants, is all."

If I were a man, I'd be thinking, here's a woman who won't be able to resist me with a gut full of tequila. And he'd be right.

Not that I need tequila to fall into bed with him. But last time, dinner and drinks turned into a night of naked fun, and I'm expecting much of the same tonight.

"A jug of margaritas, three glasses, and a round of tequila shots, please. Top shelf."

Yep, he's definitely thinking like a man.

"Ben, this is Sophia," Gabe introduces us, and I offer my hand to greet him.

"Lovely to meet you, Ben. How do you two know each other?"

He takes my hand and pulls me closer to kiss my cheek.

Oh yes, a real ladies' man, indeed.

This blue-eyed, blond, six-foot hunk of muscle is a woman pleaser in the evenings and a heartbreaker in the mornings. Mark my words, I see the type daily.

"Ben and I met at college our first year. He started out as a business major and switched to sports management when he realized he had a shot at being the best damn linebacker Columbia had ever seen."

"You play football?"

A painful expression crosses his face as he rubs at his shoulder. "Not since college, no."

Sensing this is an uncomfortable topic of conversation, I point to the shots in the center of the table. "Let's do it."

They both laugh, and Gabe passes one to Ben and me.

"Ben was drafted, and in a pre-season game, was stretchered off after an explosive defensive tackle."

"Sorry to hear that," I offer meaningfully, sprinkling salt on my wrist in preparation for my tequila.

"Yeah, reconstructive surgery with complications that followed put me out of the game. Now I run a sports shop and commentate college games for Columbia."

"Not a bad gig, at least you're still involved in what you love."

He raises his glass. "Cheers."

All three of us sink our shots like pros and move on from football and broken dreams.

An hour later, the after-work crowd filters in, and we're cramming the space between where we sit outside and the bar. Thank fuck for table service. Music from the jukebox fills the area, and Ben and I are deep in conversation about what makes the perfect first date. Gabe is silently watching the both of us, his eyes never wandering far from me.

A few hours pass, and I wish I'd kept my mouth shut about shopping tomorrow. Sharing a giant plate of chicken nachos with an extra side of jalapeños did little to help ward off the effects of the shots and numerous jugs of margaritas.

I predict my morning will include Advil and a greasy room-service breakfast. "It's the city that never sleeps, so you'll have plenty of time to shop after you've recovered," Gabe assures me as we wrap up the night, and he settles the monstrous bill.

I briefly recall making our way to Henry on the street and waving goodbye to Ben. Now, I'm waking up as we pull into my hotel. With my head resting on Gabe's shoulder, I swipe the corner of my mouth with my hand, and he laughs hysterically.

"You were snoring when you weren't talking in your sleep. Drool is the least of your concern."

Slapping at him playfully, I groan at the throbbing pain in my head. When Gabe lifts me from the back seat and throws me over his shoulder, I struggle to avoid losing the contents of my stomach all over him.

"Give me five minutes. I'll tuck her in and be right back." He must be talking to Henry, but he's not going anywhere.

"I'll need more than five minutes from you, mister."

"Yeah, and I'll give you every minute you deserve

when you're not so drunk."

Laughing at my hair falling past his ass as he carries me, my buttocks in the air past God-knows-who in the lobby, I groan. "I'm not drunk, I'm plastered."

Gabe chuckles, his shoulders jumping about beneath my stomach.

And that's where my night ends. The next thing I know, I'm waking up in bed.

Alone.

And hungover as fuck.

SOPHIA

A greasy room-service breakfast, relaxing bubble bath, and a few bottles of cold water later, I'm ready to hit the shops. Poor Henry has his work cut out for him as he drops me off and returns many times to collect my shopping bags before I'm ready to call it a day.

I haven't heard from Gabe all day, though Henry hinted at a Broadway show tonight, which I'm more than prepared for with my latest haul. Thankfully, Henry and the bellhop assist in delivering all my bags to my room, where I promptly kick off my heels and throw myself face first onto the bed.

Knackered. As. Fuck.

Confident I'm not cut out for the city which never sleeps, I set my alarm, strip out of my clothes, and snuggle beneath the quilt. An hour's nap won't hurt.

I'm on vacation, after all.

Drifting off, I startle minutes later, waking to the sound of my phone. An incoming call, not my alarm, I figure, since snoozing it doesn't work.

"Hello?" I yawn into the phone and instantly sit up. Forgetting to check the caller ID before I answered, I hope it's not a client or a business call. I *never* answer the phone so casually or when I'm half asleep.

"Sleeping beauty, get your sexy ass up and ready. We have pre-drinks, an early dinner, and a show to attend."

"Ugh, hello to you, too," I drawl, less than enthusiastic despite how wonderful the evening sounds.

Gabe chuckles at my petty whine. "Maybe I should let you sleep an extra half hour. You're going to need all your energy tonight."

Climbing out of bed, I make my way into the bathroom to turn on the hair straightener. "Let me guess... your golden plan is to seduce your way into my bed tonight."

"Yours or mine, doesn't matter. But it's happening, and tomorrow we're spending the day exploring the city."

Cocky fucker.

And fuck, cocky looks so damn good on him.

After my first Broadway show, we meet up with Ben and his date for the night at a nearby club. We dance, we laugh, and drink way too much. But with all the dance moves we're busting out, getting wasted isn't on the agenda tonight. It's been years since I last entered a club, and I'd forgotten how much I enjoy letting my hair down.

"I think you should take me home before my body is deprived of energy completely."

"Mmm, I love it when you beg."

I swat him playfully. "Believe me, you've not seen anything yet."

A throaty laugh has me biting my lip when he adds, "Oh, I'm going to make you beg for mercy tonight, sweetheart."

We wave goodbye to Ben and Amy and flee the club like two horny teenagers on a curfew. Gabe's place is closer than my hotel, and the clock is ticking. Ten minutes later, Henry drops us off, and we scramble into the apartment building.

Gabe enters his access code to his top-level penthouse, and damn, what's with elevators and this guy? Grasping his belt, I tug him close to me and unbuckle his pants. After I release his semi-hard cock, I take him in my hands.

Slowly, I glide my fisted palm up and down his length. "Does this elevator open directly into your penthouse?" When he nods, I kneel before him and keep my eyes focused on his, loving the deep shade of brown they turn when he's aroused.

He weaves his hands through my hair—a sweaty mangled mess from dancing—as I lick the tip of his cock, desperate to taste his arousal. Teasing his impressive length with my tongue, he grows harder in my grasp, and wetness pools between my thighs.

Impatiently, Gabe guides my mouth over the head of his cock and down his shaft. I hold onto his thighs for stability, taking him deeper, swirling my tongue back and forward.

Sucking his throbbing head, I torment him with pleasurable licks while my hands work him into a frenzy. Moving up and down his shaft, my mouth wet and needy, his hips rock forward, mirroring my movement.

"I'm so close, Soph. Gonna come in your mouth, sweetheart."

Silently, I nod, my eyes pleading with him to give me everything. My nails dig into his thighs once again as I pleasure him with my dirty mouth alone. His pace quickens, and I match the rhythm.

"Fuuuck!" Gabe holds my head still, his cock deep in my throat as he spills his seed into my mouth.

Unsure when the elevator doors opened, his suite awaits as he pulls me to my feet. "That mouth of yours is sinfully delicious. But for the rest of the night, I'm in charge."

My body hums with anticipation. Gabe guides me through the expansive living area into a massive room to the right. A super-sized king bed with dark wooden posts sits in the center of the area overlooking the city lights through the floor-to-ceiling windows. My mouth drops at the beauty before me, briefly forgetting where I am.

"Get naked."

Gabe commands my attention, and I obey without hesitation.

First, I begin by removing my jewelry, each movement slow and seductive. Watching me intently, he steps in behind me and carefully releases the zipper on my dress. "Thank you," I whisper, turning to him.

Silently retreating to the corner of the room, he sits casually in the armchair, now naked from the waist up. Eyes glued to me, he removes his shoes and socks, and I remain focused on his attentiveness as I step out of my dress.

In my brand-new lingerie purchase—sapphire blue satin thong set, lined with black lace, and my Jimmy Choo's—I stand before him. The power I hold over him at this moment intensifies my need to satisfy him.

To satisfy his every desire.

"Keep going," he growls, his glare burning deep into my chest.

When I move to step out of my heels, his words stop me. "No. The heels stay."

With slow, deliberate hands, I remove my bra and toss it to the side. I watch Gabe absentmindedly lick his lips, his eyes hooded with lust. With superb balance, I lower my thong, and step out, throwing them at him. His nostrils flare, but he doesn't move.

"Lay on the bed, your wet pussy facing me."

Turned on by his request, I position myself on his bed and drop my knees to the side, opening myself completely to him. His greedy eyes zero in on my glistening, naked lips, and I wait.

He watches silently.

"Play with your clit, Sophia."

Finally, he stands where I can see him better. He steps toward me but remains out of reach. Pushing his pants and boxers to the floor, he flicks them to the side with his foot. His cock is hard once more as he wraps his fist around himself.

Gliding my finger through the wetness of my folds, I cover my clit in my juices. Exposed before him, I lie naked, and continue to massage my nerve center, desperate for the feel of his cock inside me.

"Gabe," I moan, watching his wrist flex with each of his fluid movements.

My hips flex unintentionally, seeking more. "Stay still."

Pre-cum drops from the head of his cock, and I lose all focus. My hips writhe against my fingertips, and he lets out a growl.

"Roll over, knees spread on the edge of the bed."

Lord have mercy. This man is going to kill me. My body screams for—

"Fuck!" I barely position myself when he drives his cock deep inside, remaining still until my walls stretch to accommodate his girth.

"That what you wanted?"

"Ye... yes."

My body quivers as he withdraws and slams into me once again. I close my eyes, hanging my head between my elbows, pushing back for more. Gabe circles his hips, the tip of his cock teasing my G-spot with every circular motion. Reaching over me, he clutches my hair and rips my head back.

Wet lips kiss their way down my back as he plays with me, teasing my entrance with his tip and pulling out. Over and over, he repeats it until I can't take it any longer.

This time, he inches forward, and I slam myself back over his cock. The force knocks the wind from me. His grip on my hair intensifies, and his other hand slaps my ass.

Hard.

Yelping at the unexpected sting, I hover on the

edge of ecstasy.

"If you want my cock, you're going to have to beg for it."

Men don't hold a high enough place in my life to beg them for anything. But *fuck,* I'm not above begging when it comes to sex with Gabe *fucking* Lugreno.

"Please, Gabe. I need you."

"No, Sophia. You don't *need* me. You *want* my cock. Say it."

"No. I *need* your cock so fucking bad it hurts."

He slaps his palm over my other cheek and pulls away, flipping me to my back.

His hooded stare pins me to the bed. Running his finger through my folds, he dares me to beg as if my life depends on it.

And I do.

My God, do I beg.

Until fucking him is the only thing on my mind.

"Now, Gabe. Please. Fuck me like you mean it. I can't..."

Yes.

In one fierce effort, he fills my core and triggers a tidal wave of pent-up frustration.

My body quakes beneath him as he slams into me precisely and perfectly.

"Come with me, sweetheart. I want to feel you explode on my cock."

"Oh fuck, Gabe."

My world splinters, my mind alters, and my body crumples as we ride out our earth-shattering climax together.

Chapter 8

SOPHIA
Six Weeks Later - August

"Gabe, what are you doing here?"

As I enter my office, I find him sprawled out over my sofa as if he belongs there. His tie hanging loose around his neck, his hair disheveled, and that fuck-me grin he wears unknowingly thrusting me into a dangerous place.

Kelli is on the phone at her desk when I glare at her through my glass wall.

"How the hell did you make it past the front desk?"

"Flattery gets you everywhere, Sophia. Even Kelli isn't immune to my charm." He winks, standing to approach me and delivers a quick kiss on my cheek. Shoving him off a moment too late, his woody masculine scent fills my senses, and on weak and shaky legs, I round the desk to take a seat.

Distance is my friend.

My breathing is uneven, and my words fail to deliver the impact of the emotions I'm experiencing.

"You can't show up at my place of business unannounced, and for fuck's sake, don't act like we're something we're not."

Gabe chuckles and pulls up a seat across from me. I grip the edge of my desk so tight I fear my nails will leave imprints in the solid timber. "What we're not is strangers. I'm in town securing a business deal and want to take you to dinner."

"I'm busy."

"Yes, you are. I checked your schedule with Kelli, and she blocked out tonight from eight o'clock on. I'll have a car pick you up."

"I'm more than capable of finding my way." I level him with a glare. "I don't require a car or driver."

Gabe grins, his dreamy eyes glittering in the fluorescent lighting. "That's not a no to dinner. I'll see you there."

He moves to leave, my head a whirlwind of frustration.

"Mr. Lugreno."

My words stop him dead in his tracks. Slowly, he turns to me, his gaze piercing mine.

I gulp.

I'm not one to be intimidated by a man, much less one who's younger than me. And money does nothing for me. God knows my fortune probably matches his own, regardless of whether I choose to flaunt it. But Gabe's stare has me rethinking what I was about to say.

"Where's there?"

"You ask too many questions, Sophia. My driver will collect you from your apartment." With that, he stalks out of my office, past Kelli, who's staring after him with wide eyes.

"Kelli!" I screech from behind my desk.

Sheepishly, Kelli steps into my office. It's not normal for me to chastise my employees, but this is Kelli, my best friend and partner in crime. "What the fuck, Kel?"

"I can explain," she rushes, taking a seat.

"I'm waiting."

"He called earlier when you were in a meeting to check your availability for a dinner meeting. I didn't know he was coming in this afternoon."

"Why was he waiting in my office?"

"He insisted."

Of course, he did. The entitled bastard.

"Are you..."

"Mad? Working? Busy? Yes, all of the above."

Kelli nods, her expression serious. "I'll be at my desk if you need me."

"Kelli," I say as she's halfway through the door.

"How does he know where I live?"

She cringes. "I only gave him the street address to the apartment block."

Waving her off, I'm annoyed with the unexpected visit more than her giving out information she shouldn't have.

No idea where we're going or what Gabe's game plan is, I dress as I would for any meeting with a client. I watch from inside the foyer of my apartment building for a town car to pull to the curb before I make my way outside. "Enjoy your evening, Sophia."

I smile at Saul, the concierge. "Always do."

Viktor is waiting with the door open, happy to usher me in as I approach the vehicle. "Hello again, Miss Evans." I nod politely and scoot into the back seat, shocked to find Gabe isn't here.

As we pull out into the traffic, I quiz Viktor unsuccessfully, "Where's Mr. Lugreno?"

"Waiting patiently for your arrival, Miss Evans."

It's been six weeks since my weekend in New York, where we agreed to leave things open but casual between us. His showing up today, unannounced and requesting my presence for dinner isn't my idea of casual.

We pull into the pier. Gabe stands waiting for our arrival with a bottle of bubbly and two glasses, dressed more casually than usual in jeans and a royal blue dress shirt rolled to his elbows. Until

Gabe, I've never been a fan of rolled-up sleeves, but this man and his chiseled forearms—they're too perfect to be covered.

Exiting the car and waving goodbye to Viktor, I marvel at the idea of taking a cruise on the River Thames. "Thank you for joining me," Gabe says, pulling me to him. With a gesture as grand as a river cruise, I can hardly deny him now, can I?

"Kiss me as if you miss me," he growls, owning my lips before I can answer.

The sun setting in the distance, our river boat waiting, and bubbly at his side, I embrace his need for me. Our tongues dance as I press my body to him, my hands clutching his collar.

Music from the boat wafts across the pier, and we pull apart, my mind dizzy with desire.

"I didn't miss you one bit," I smirk, taking my glass from him.

"I noticed," he groans wryly.

Two hours of dancing as we glide down the river overlooking the beautiful London cityscape at night has to be one of the most romantic dates. I need to suggest this more often to my clients. Eating canapes and sipping fruity bubbles over casual chit-chat with other diners and the ambiance of a great local jazz band is surprisingly good for the soul.

The night air is cool when we pull back into the pier, and I see Viktor waiting for us in the distance.

As we thank our waiters and the hosts of the evening, I tuck myself beneath Gabe's arm and crush against his side for added warmth. "Take me home?" I say, glancing up at him with a grin.

He brushes a kiss on the top of my head. "I thought you'd never ask."

Chuckling, I dig my shoulder playfully into his ribs. "Like you'd have it any other way."

"You know me too well already."

He's only in town for one night before flying to Argentina for a meeting, and I'm damn sure going to get my fill of him before he leaves again.

SOPHIA
Two Months Later - October

"You're late."

"Hello, brother, lovely to see you too." I accept a kiss on the cheek from my eldest sibling, Roman, who's comfortably seated at the bar, chatting to Maxine.

"Work looks like it's kicking your ass, Soph." Max winks at me while preparing one of my favorite cocktails. She's the best mixologist in the city, and her drinks make headlines in the pub and club scene.

I sigh, knowing it's not the workload. It's the midnight calls with a certain man I wish to keep under wraps. "I look that good, huh?"

I've no doubt I'm wearing exhaustion like a crown, but what can I do? There's only so much sea kelp I can expose my skin to without growing scales and gills.

Wednesday nights at Maximum is our mid-week catch-up. I glance over to our usual booth to find my little brother, Jarett, and a few others who sometimes join us.

Taking my dirty cowboy in a boot-shaped glass to the booth, I greet everyone except Claire with a smile. I can't stand her, and despite all the history between our families, I still don't understand why she mingles with us. Or why one of us hasn't cast her to the side yet.

"How are things at the café, Roman?"

My brother is an incredible chef who opted to establish the best café in downtown London instead of opening a five-star restaurant. He's never been one for the nightlife since he outgrew his rebellion in his mid-twenties, so the hours of operation suit him better, I guess.

"Better than ever. Wait until you check out the new menu we released this week."

We often meet at Café Zest for lunches throughout the week, but I've only made it a handful of times over the past few weeks.

"Where have you been hiding out, Sophia? We haven't seen you as often as usual," Jarett grills, his eyes narrowing in on me. A dead giveaway he suspects something is up.

"Not hiding. I've been busier than a nun's vibrator."

The group roars with laughter.

"Only you, Soph. Only you." Roman shakes his head.

"Seriously, though, I'm sending out party invites soon. It's my fortieth in five months."

I eyeball everyone around the table to make sure they're listening. My birthday is important to me, and the party will be one to remember for years to come.

"As if you'd ever let us forget," Jarett chuffs.

Roman adds, "And we wouldn't miss it for the world. Are you still planning to have it here at Maximum?"

"Of course, Max is giving me friends rates on all drinks for the night."

"Huh, like you need a discount," Claire chimes in, and I do my best to ignore her unwarranted rudeness.

Focusing my attention back to Jarett, I ask, "How's the gallery chugging along?"

"Expecting a new shipment by the end of the week. Brand new artist to the gallery, and a deal I've been working on for months."

"That's brilliant, J. I'm happy for you." It's great to see him smiling, but it doesn't light up his eyes like it once did.

"Our next public showing event will be the

biggest one yet, I imagine. He's a huge name where many of my big buying clients are concerned."

The strain in his voice when he talks of his business success is evident as if he doesn't deserve the right to be happy anymore without Helena at his side.

Despite my best efforts to get him appointments with the finest grief therapists in the country, he's determined to ride the wave of despair and loss on his own.

Maxine delivers another round of drinks to the table and tells me she's working on a new cocktail for my themed party, which I've not yet disclosed to anyone but her. "I'm excited to see what you come up with. And you better not be working the event yourself! I want you to be partying with me."

"Already organized the night off. I'll be partying like there's no tomorrow." She winks, making me grin like a fool.

"Will you be bringing a date?" Claire, the nosey bitch asks.

Roman laughs from the opposite side of the table. "Max doesn't have time to date."

Oh, it seems I may have put my foot in my mouth without realizing it.

Max and Roman's yo-yo *friends with benefits* is rarely discussed, and for the most part, never thought of as part of our lives. Until a moment like this when animosity arises between them, and it's difficult to miss.

"It's too far away to say for sure, but I expect so, yes."

Her answer leaves Roman chewing on the inside of his lip, his expression solemn.

When Max returns to the bar and peeks over at our booth, I offer her an apologetic grin, and she waves me off.

"What about you, Sophia. Bringing a date to your party?" Claire asks without bothering to look my way. If she could take her filthy mind off my baby brother for more than five minutes, I'd be a little more receptive to her. I can all but hear her mind ticking over, waiting to pounce when Jarett shows the first sign of coming out of his grieving period.

"A real woman never tells."

The truth is, I don't know if Gabe will be around by then or if the midnight calls and international fling will be a thing of the past come March. And I don't need a man on my arm. I'm the party, and I'll be the center of attention with or without Gabe.

Or anyone else.

Tonight, though, I'm happy to sit back and enjoy an evening of banter and fine cocktails with the people I value most in my life.

Chapter 10

SOPHIA
Two Months Later – December

"I'm heading out early. Do you need anything from me before I leave?"

Kelli shakes her head. "No, everything is under control. Are you still taking the full weekend off?"

She's the only one who knows my weekend plans do *not* include a conference of any kind.

"Yes, I doubt I'll be contactable, so I'm leaving my life's work in your capable hands."

"I still don't understand why you didn't suggest going away next weekend instead. You could've stayed the week up until Christmas as we'll be closed anyway."

"Trust me, two nights is more than enough for what we have planned."

"Dirty whore," she jokes, and I shrug happily,

owning the compliment as it was intended.

More than two nights in a romantic city with Gabe is too much to comprehend for this happily single, almost forty-year-old.

Three hours later, Gabe and I are on his private Jet, bound for Paris. He flew direct from New York to collect me for a secret, dirty weekend in my favorite city in the world. In less than an hour, we'll arrive and settle into our hotel.

And if I have anything to say about it, we won't leave our room until we're required to check out and dive back into reality.

"I notice you packed on the lighter side... are you planning on staying in all weekend?" A cheeky grin spreads across his face.

Laughing, I raise my glass of champagne to his in a toast. "I believe that's the plan, yes."

Gabe chuckles knowingly, rubbing his hand up the length of my thigh, teasing me with his light touch.

As we're both familiar with Paris, we have no plans to do any sightseeing. Apart from meals, we have no desire to leave the room. In case we get carried away, Gabe booked a suite in a hotel with the best-rated twenty-four-hour room service.

My luggage exists of three outfits and, dare I say, only two pairs of shoes and an assortment of sexy lingerie. My intentions are clear based on what I've packed.

Maci Dillon

"Does it turn you on, sneaking around like this?" He leans forward, his hand snaking beneath my skirt, his finger teasing the wet fabric of my panties.

"We're not sneaking around."

"No? Where did you tell your friends you were going this weekend?"

Unable to resist, I lean toward him as his lips kiss their way up my neck until goosebumps break out over my skin. With a firm hand, he pushes my legs open, and glances up at me, waiting for an answer.

"To Paris for a training seminar."

Gabe laughs, his eyes never leaving mine. He drags me forward, my pussy on the edge of the seat, and kneels on the floor. As he pulls my panties to the side, he dives between my thighs, and closes his lips around my clit. Good God, this man and his magic tongue. In seconds, I'm writhing over his mouth, grinding my wet pussy against his face, about to experience my first mile-high orgasm.

"Yes, Gabe..." I whisper, wrapping my legs over his shoulders. "So fucking good," I moan, on the cusp of no return.

My body shudders as he holds my hips tightly in place, pressed against him as he nips and sucks, swirling his tongue over my clit as if he's starving for the last taste of perfection.

My fingers rake through his hair, clutching his thick strands as I lose all control and give in to the pleasure only Gabe can offer.

70

Tenderly, he licks every last drop of arousal from me, moaning as he keeps me pinned in place, his fingertips digging into my buttocks.

I'm his to devour.

His to cherish.

With dark eyes, hooded and drunk with lust, he pushes back on the balls of his feet and stands above me. My mouth, level with his groin, waters at the sight of the bulge in his jeans. Slowly, he unbuckles his belt, pops the button, and lowers the zipper. Reaching out, I tug at the denim and his boxers, pulling them down his hips until he's fully revealed to me.

Desperate to taste his arousal, I lick my lips. A bead of pre-cum pools on the head of his cock, begging to be licked. I take his length in my hand, teasing him with slow, purposeful strokes until he pushes my hand away and pulls me abruptly from my seat.

He spins me around so my back is facing him, my arms resting over the top of the seat. Hitching my skirt up around my waist, he shuffles my hips back toward the edge and pulls my thong down. Teasing my entrance with his cock, he asks, "How do you feel about an audience?"

Confused, I turn and shoot him a questionable look. He forces me back into position, ignoring my glare. That's when I see the young man who I saw up front with the pilot when I first arrived, step from behind the curtain, separating us from the front of the jet. The exact moment Gabe enters me from behind, I gasp at the intrusion.

"Gabe?" His name gushes out as a question, and my body tenses with the addition of an audience. Is this what Gabe was referring to? Reeling, I push back, unsure if he's aware of our visitor.

"Lenny, I'm glad you made it," Gabe welcomes him. The intruder's eyes are steadfast and narrowed in on me. "I want you to watch me fuck Sophia... her punishment for keeping me from her friends and family."

The guy moves toward us, and Gabe stops him, not missing a beat as he rotates his hips at a steady pace, teasing me with what's to come. "Don't move any closer. And don't touch yourself. Just watch me pleasure my woman."

His woman.

"Why are you doing this, Gabe?"

"Don't pretend it bothers you, sweetheart. Your dam burst wide open the moment he walked in. You secretly love an audience," he whispers over my shoulder.

"I... I don't know," I gush. It's a new-to-me experience, but I can't argue.

As Gabe squeezes my thighs and pumps himself deeper inside me, I know I'm not opposed to being watched. My nipples harden in the confines of my bra, my shirt still in place, concealing me from view.

And I wish I were naked.

Each time Gabe flexes his hips, his reach deepens, and it's not long before I'm pushing against him, looking for more.

I feel him everywhere.

Overwhelming my senses.

Pulling me to him in ways I've never known.

When I rest my forehead on the chair's headrest, Gabe orders me to focus on Lenny as he watches us. His voice is rough and equally as turned on as I am.

And fuck, if it doesn't arouse me even more.

As I watch Lenny's cock grow, stretching his pants, it pleases me knowing he'll never be where Gabe is—deep inside me, bringing my body to the brink of eruption and owning my orgasms the way he does.

Because whether I acknowledge it out loud or not, my body belongs to this man. Nobody has ever pleasured me the way he does. His bossy asshole attitude is growing on me too.

"Focus." Gabe slaps my ass.

My pussy clenches tightly around his cock, and he groans, slapping me again. I cry out, my eyes meeting Lenny's as his mouth drops open the slightest bit.

"Sir?"

"No, Lenny, you watch her until she explodes around my cock, then leave."

Lenny nods, not taking his eyes off me.

Gabe moves quicker and penetrates me harder until my eyes are rolling back in my head, and I'm gasping his name like he's the god I've always dreamed of.

And he is.

SOPHIA
Three Months Later - March

"I think we should tell your brothers about us before your party next weekend."

Pausing with my fork full of brisket midway to my mouth, I frown. "Tell them what?"

I imagine the awkward conversation with my brothers over for dinner, where I introduce Gabe as my casual fling and the man who'll be accompanying me to my birthday celebrations.

Yeah, not going to happen.

"You obviously don't care about me meeting them, or I wouldn't be attending. So, what is it, Sophia?"

I grunt, irritated by the direction of the conversation.

"Can't we enjoy our meal and celebrate my last

night with you in my thirties?" I'm not beyond whining to get out of having this discussion tonight or any other.

"Of course, sweetheart."

If I were a glass of wine, I'd be pouring over with gratitude. My birthday might be a week away but Gabe flew in today and will be gone in less than twenty-four hours. I won't see him again until the day of my birthday and I'll be fucked if I'm going to spend that time hashing out my sex life with my brothers.

"Thank you."

Gabe lowers his fork and tops up our glasses.

"As soon as you answer the question."

Fuck.

How do I politely tell him I'm not interested in a meet-the-family situation?

Not now, not ever.

"We're fucking, Gabe. Why do we need to meet with them privately to disclose it? They'll assume that all on their own when you show up with me." His gaze drops at my words, and I instantly wish I'd thought before I'd spoken.

"Trust me, they won't be expecting me to bring a date, even for my birthday party. To my family and most of my friends, I'm the epitome of a spinster. I wouldn't be surprised if they have a delivery of cats sent to my apartment for when I return home from the party."

I offer a laugh to lighten the mood, but Gabe has disengaged.

After spending my days and many nights setting up couples for meet and greets, which often turn into happily ever afters, my personal dating life is non-existent.

Except for my casual fling with Gabe while he's in the country.

And the weekends when he picks me up and treats me to a few nights in Paris.

Or the few times I've flown to meet him in New York for a quick visit.

Gah.

"The point is, I'm not looking for whatever this is to change anytime soon."

"So, you still want to pass this off as a casual fuck?"

As I glance around the restaurant, I'm grateful we're situated far enough away that other diners will not overhear.

"Isn't that exactly what this is, Gabe? We've never discussed anything different."

I'm confused by his sudden push for this to be more.

"It's been almost a year since we met at the gala, Sophia."

"And what a great year it's been. I'm not denying I enjoy spending time with you, Gabe, but why change something that's working?"

"Maybe this no-fucks-given attitude toward our relationship isn't working for me anymore."

A waiter scoots past our table on his way to a nearby table when Gabe flags him down and requests a whiskey for himself and a Cosmo for me. "What are you saying, Gabe?"

Holding my breath, I wait for the words I'm sure will follow. He wants to end this.

"I'm saying I want more than a casual fling with you, Sophia. Is that too much to ask?"

No, it's not.

But anything more than what we have is knocking on the door of commitment and asking for heartbreak to follow.

I never imagined tonight I would be breaking up with my billionaire fling because of a fear of commitment and having to buy batteries on my way home.

Alone.

"As far as I see it, next Saturday night you'll be the man on my arm... my date and the sexiest man in the room. And I'm willing to beat off any women with a stick if they try to seduce you on the dance floor."

Mr. Broody delivers a smirk. "Would fighting for my attention make you jealous, sweetheart?"

Not that I've considered this before, but yes, it would, and I tell him so.

"Fine, you win. Only because it's you're focused on your birthday celebrations, but this discussion isn't over."

Nodding, I share a grateful smile with him. In other words, we'll soon revisit the conversation and decide on a label for our relationship or part ways.

Neither of which I'm particularly happy about.

After spending the morning with Kassidy—Jarett's one and only fling, whose holiday turned into a twelve-month stay—shopping for her costume for my party, followed by a pampering session with my girls in preparation for my big night tomorrow, I treat myself to an early night, knowing Gabe will be on his way to me shortly.

"Hi sweetheart," he answers my phone call.

Yawning as I sprawl out in bed, he laughs. "Sounds like I'm keeping you up. How was your day with the girls?"

"Freaking fan-tabulous! But I'm knackered. Are you coming here or going to your hotel when you arrive?"

There's a brief pause on the end of the line. "I didn't know that was an option. You've never allowed me to spend the night at your apartment before."

"Technically, it won't be the whole night as you don't arrive until the early hours of the morning." I chuckle nervously, unsure why I even expected him to come to me. Or why I suddenly want to be his first call when he arrives.

"I'd love—"

I cut him off, on the brink of an emotional freak-out. "Never mind, I need my beauty sleep, it's probably best to see you in the morning, after your meeting."

"As you wish, Sophia. Goodnight."

"Goodnight, Gabe."

GABE

I arrived at two in the morning on the red-eye, slept a few hours and met with Kassidy, my new hire for a project I'm working on with Jarett, Sophia's brother. As soon as I leave our meeting, I all but run to Sophia, desperate to see my birthday girl.

When I show up at her apartment an hour earlier than expected, Sophia leaps into my arms and I never want to let her go.

"I missed you too, sweetheart."

She squints at me. "I never said I missed you."

Laughing, Sophia pulls me inside and kisses me fiercely.

"So, tell me about your meeting with your new contractor. Everything go as planned?"

"It did. I'm comfortable I've made the right decision. She's perfect for this new project."

Sophia gives me the ideal opportunity to tell her I'm working with her brother on this project, and I fail to mention it. Why, I don't know.

I'd planned to tell her so many times prior to today, and it's part of the reason I mentioned wanting to meet with Roman and Jarett before the party. The awkward turn in the conversation when I brought it up last week, had me thinking better of it.

Worst case scenario, tonight may be our last night together, but I doubt Sophia is that petty. It's not as if my business colleagues are something we discuss. But the thought of Sophia not being part of my life causes an ache in an unfamiliar part of my chest.

My only plan for today is to seduce the woman I'm falling for, to own her body in a way she knows she belongs to me.

And me alone.

Before I make my intentions clear to her family. *Tonight.*

Which, against my better judgment, should've been done before tonight. To say Sophia's brothers welcome me with open arms at her party is a stretch.

As Sophia and I descend the stairs at the speakeasy, I catch a glimpse of Jarett by the bar. He stands beside a man I assume to be Roman. And I nearly trip as I recognize the woman at Jarett's side as Kassidy, my new hire, dressed in a barely-there corset.

Sophia squeezes my arm, bringing my attention back to her as we near the bottom step. Dressed as she requested as a twenty's gangster, she outshines me in her whorish outfit—a sequin-covered gold corset—deliciously curvy and busty—a head of jewels, and her brown hair pinned up in a bob.

As we step into the limelight, I remove my hat and glance around the room, proud to be at Sophia's side. The shock on Jarett and Kassidy's faces is a look I'll never forget. And regretfully, it could've been avoided.

"Presenting to you, Ms. Sophia Evans accompanied this evening by Mr. Gabe Lugreno. Please raise your glasses for a toast. Happy birthday, Lady Sophia, and congratulations on forty fabulous years. May the next forty be equally as brilliant."

Not only is Jarett pissed that I arrived with his sister, but it was a surprise to all of us that his girlfriend, Kassidy, is the one and the same who now works for me.

If I were honest with Sophia about my business with Jarett and if she had agreed to let us meet before the party, the Kassidy situation wouldn't have come as such a shock on the night we were supposed to be celebrating Sophia's fabulous forty years.

The night passes too quickly despite the awkward beginning. Sophia introduces me to everyone as her date, although I don't have the opportunity to catch up with Kassidy or Jarett again, and every time I get near Roman our moment is cut short.

I'm happy for a taste of what's to come if Sophia ever accepts me as more than a casual fuck. I can see myself in her life and will do anything to be the man at her side through her next forty years.

Weeks have passed since I was last in London but tonight is the annual gala and one year since I first laid eyes on Sophia in the flesh. The internet photos, while beautiful, didn't do her any justice, and she's grown even more beautiful these past twelve months as she has edged her way into my heart, whether she likes it or not.

"What are you thinking about?" Sophia loops her

arm in mine when I return to her side now that her brothers have walked away. She's proudly watching the crowd mingling in the ballroom with Kassidy by her side, unaware of my presence.

"I was remembering our brief introduction in this exact ballroom at last year's gala and thinking how different we are today."

"Oh please, spare me the romantic bullshit. The only difference is you wanted to fuck me then, and now you are."

A throaty chuckle bubbles up, and I slap her ass. The sudden movement as she jolts forward alerts Kassidy to my arrival. "Gabe." She smiles. "I didn't realize you were in town. Are we set to start on the contract?"

Before I have a chance to answer, Jarett and Roman arrive at her side with *what-the-fuck is he doing here* expressions on their faces.

Welcome to my world.

A world where I not only have to fight for Sophia's love but for the acceptance of her overprotective brothers as well.

Jarett acknowledges me with a slight nod, lacing his arm around Kassidy's waist, pulling her tightly toward him as if I might take off with her if given the chance.

Sophia's entire demeanor changes once they join us, and I hate it. She appears nervous, ready to flee the conversation at the first opportunity. That's until I respond to Kassidy's question, "This trip is all pleasure."

My arm rests across Sophia's back, and my hand sits protectively on her hip. She nestles closer, and my heart dances when she smiles up at me, her eyes filled with more emotion than I've seen from her so far.

I continue explaining how it's been a year since we originally met, and Jarett's broodiness kicks up a notch. His glare directed at me alone. "So, you two have been dating for a whole year?"

Gritting my teeth, I refrain from causing a scene when I answer *yes,* and Sophia simultaneously says *no.*

"Okay, well, this has been lovely. When do the auctions begin, Sophia?" Kassidy assists with a swift change of subject.

"Yes, I should get a move on," Sophia responds. "This event won't run itself. Thank you all for being here." She smiles at everyone and shocks the fuck out of me as she pulls me in for a heated kiss and leaves the four of us staring at each other.

"I trust this won't be awkward for you, Jarett, with us being in business together. Or for you, Kassidy."

"You mean the fact you're fucking my sister?"

A grin pulls at my lips in response to his avid distaste of the situation. "Expect to be seeing a lot more of me."

Roman frowns and tucks his free hand into the pocket of his trousers, his expression solemn.

"Sophia's not the dating type, so whatever you're thinking, don't," Jarett spits back at me.

"I meet a lot of women on my travels, but none who have affected me like Sophia. She may not realize it yet, but we're meant to be together."

Roman and Jarett laugh while Kassidy offers a hint of a smile.

"Mark my words... I'll do whatever it takes to make her mine."

Chapter 12

SOPHIA

My incessant alarm wakes me from my slumber.

When it abruptly stops and starts again, I'm awake enough to recognize it's my phone ringing, not my alarm. It's Sunday and it was almost sunrise by the time we fell asleep. I roll over to find Gabe missing and his side of the bed is cold. The first night I allow him to stay in my apartment, and he flees before I wake.

I huff, making my way out of bed to the shower. When drying myself, my phone buzzes again, and the front door of my apartment slams shut. "Hello?" I call out, unsure what the fuck is going on.

What sounds like the blinds are being pulled in the living area echoes into my room. "Hey, babe, it's me. I went for coffee." Gabe enters the bathroom with a strange expression on his face.

"What's wrong?" An uncomfortable feeling replaces the exhaustion I woke with.

"Get dressed, we need to talk."

"About what? What's going on, Gabe?"

I follow him into the living area bathed in darkness when the morning sun should be filtering through. My phone continues to ring in the bedroom, but my feet won't carry me to pick it up. My heart threatens to lurch from my chest, the all-too-familiar feeling of bad news on the doorstep. That's when I notice the newspaper on the bench, and gravity pulls me to it.

My gaze follows Gabe as he retreats to the bedroom, returning moments later with my phone in hand as I pick up the paper. "I think you should take a seat, Sophia, before you open that."

With shaky hands, I take my phone from Gabe and notice missed calls from Jarett, Roman, Maxine, and Kelli, plus many unknown numbers which are cause enough for concern.

As I unfold the *Daily News,* I take a seat and my eyes widen in shock. My mouth falls open—it's dry, and I gasp for air as if an elephant is sitting on my chest, squeezing the life out of me.

The headline reads, *Billionaire Sophia Evans Caught Sleeping with Clients.*

The front page is a collage of images of Gabe and me together, leaving his hotel, dancing at the gala benefit last night, and behind closed doors at

Incontro. The largest is of us walking hand in hand into my apartment in the wee hours of this morning.

How the fuck did they even have time to print and distribute this?

The earlier blanket of fear wrapping its ugliness around me turns to anger. Violation of my personal life is one thing, but false accusations made public that threaten to tear apart my empire are beyond fucked up.

Gabe stands peering out the window as I put two and two together and join him at his side. He pulls me into the crook of his arm, his strong hold is somewhat of a comfort as I peel back the blinds to reveal a media frenzy below us at the entrance of my apartment.

"This can't be happening, Gabe," I whisper as tears form in my eyes. Gabe turns to me and pulls me in for a crushing hug, squeezing the last of my angst-filled breath from my body.

"I hate to say it, but I may or may not have made things worse when I went out for coffee."

"How is that possible? Do you not understand what they're accusing me of?" We have contracts in place for protecting our clients, lengthy legal documents outlining every possible definition and example of sexual harassment and more. Now I've been accused of sleeping with a client, which goes against everything I personally believe and all the causes I publicly advocate for—child slavery, sexual assault, and workplace harassment.

No, it couldn't possibly get any worse, no matter what he thinks he's done.

"These photos are all of us, Gabe. And you're not, nor have you ever been, a client of mine."

Fuck.

The day I asked Kelli to look into him, had she missed something?

Of course not. Running a name through the database pulls any information for current and past clients, including close contacts.

Loud banging on the door tears my focus from the clusterfuck at hand. I march toward the intrusive sound but Gabe cuts me off and pulls open the door. He looks ready to pounce, but Jarett rushes him the moment he sets eyes on him.

"What the fuck have you done, asshole?" Jarett grabs Gabe by the shirt collar and plows him roughly into the wall.

"Enough!" I scold them both as Kassidy rushes past to show her support in a bone-crushing hug.

"Why didn't you answer my calls, Sophia? I've been worried sick." Jarett pulls me into a comforting embrace, and I allow him.

"I woke up to the phone, and by the time I showered and got my wits about me, Gabe was back with the newspaper, shutting this place up like Fort Knox."

"Why, so he can hide from what he's done?" Jarett looks pissed, and I'm confused as to what the fuck is going on.

"Tell me what the fuck you've done, Gabe."

His usual cocky grin falls and is replaced with a stern look. I'm looking between the three of them when Gabe's gaze falls back on me. "I did it to protect you. I figure if the press think we're in a committed relationship, this whole frenzy will turn in a different direction."

"How committed, Gabe?"

"Marriage, that's how fucking committed," Jarett pipes in, his words laced with anger. Kassidy glances at me, and I stare back at her, unable to lock eyes with Gabe.

Marriage?

"I run a multi-million-dollar business, Gabe. Marriage isn't the answer. There's a reason I have always kept my personal life separate from my professional persona."

"And look how that turned out for you," Gabe spits back at me, causing me to flinch.

"It's all over the news, and they're basically broadcasting from outside your apartment. Gabe going out for coffee today is what has implicated him even further, possibly destroying your career forever, and now the bastard thinks he's going to marry you."

My face falls into my hands in despair and I make

a mental note of all my contacts with local and national media outlets. First, I know I should contact Kelli, although missed calls make me think she's aware of the situation we're facing. Next on the agenda is to call my legal team and media department.

All before my morning coffee, the day after the most successful fundraising gala I've run to date.

Jarett crosses the room and switches on the television. Immediately an image of Gabe and me at last night's event fills the screen.

Chapter 13

SOPHIA

I'm unable to leave my apartment for fear of being accosted by the paparazzi so I indulge in conference calls one after the other with my team. A team I can't help but feel I've let down and disappointed.

First, I speak with Kelli and give her a list of media contacts to reach out to on my behalf. My public relations manager, Stacy, is in damage-control mode before I get her on the phone. "Stay inside, don't answer the door, and ignore any incoming calls from numbers you don't know. I'm drafting a press release to have sent to you within the next hour." There's a pause on the line.

"What is it?"

"Forgive me, Sophia, but to do my job, I need to ask…" My eyes flutter closed in frustration.

"The entire story is bullshit. Gabe isn't a client,

never has been, and we've been seeing each other regularly for a year now."

"And you're getting married? Was this planned pre or post the reports in this morning's news?"

Groaning, I bite out what she already knows to be true. "Post. Gabe thought he was helping to save my reputation."

"I thought as much, and he might be right. Act the part, and we can weave this as an epic love story for the woman who's devoted her life's work to creating lasting love and happiness for thousands of couples."

"Huh. You think that will work?"

"I'm good, if not excellent, at what I do, Sophia. That's why you pay me the big bucks, remember?"

"Of course, you're amazing. I don't doubt your abilities."

The doubt is in my own ability to keep this under wraps and play the part of a woman in love. Over the past year, I've grown fond of Gabe and our time spent together, but love?

"I have issued a statement to all the staff. They know exactly what to say if approached by the media, and my team is working on contacting all current members to lay any concerns to rest. We've got this."

"I'm glad you do because I feel like a wrecking ball has torn a hole through my life this morning, and now, I have a fucking wedding to plan."

Stacy laughs, and I release a weak chuckle. "The plans can wait. We'll say you weren't ready to tell the world yet, and more details of your fairy-tale wedding will be some time away."

After hanging up the phone in my office, I bury my head in my hands.

What would my mother think of the mess I've made? I can't fathom the idea of a wedding and not having my parents there. As a little girl, I dreamed of the day my father would accompany me down the aisle and hand me over to my prince charming.

Except he'll never get that chance, and I don't want another man in my life who could one day be ripped away from me.

"How are you holding up?" There's a knock on the door behind me, and Kassidy steps in with a steaming hot cup of coffee.

"Oh, you know, a nervous wreck full of uncertainty and fear of losing everything I've built." I offer a weak smile, but deep down, I know it sounds worse than it is. Tomorrow, the media will find something more scandalous to share with their readers, and my so-called misdemeanor will be long forgotten.

Kassidy sits on the corner of my desk. "I don't want to leave Jarett and Gabe alone for too long, all that pent-up testosterone and stuff, but I wanted to see how you were doing."

I squeeze her hand. "Honestly, I'm fine. I could

drive a nail file through Gabe's eye for saying we're getting married, but apart from that, my team has a handle on the press issues."

"To think I'd have missed all this drama if I returned to Australia at the end of my holiday."

"Nah, even if you went home, I have no doubt you and Jarett would've found your way back to each other." It's true. My brother is one lucky son of a bitch to have Kassidy in his life.

She smiles beautifully. "Thank you."

"That said, if this clusterfuck hasn't blown over by the time your contract is up, I might move back to Oz with you." Laughing, it dawns on me, if that were to happen, Jarett would likely pack up his life and cross the ocean with her.

"Stop. You're overthinking it. We all agreed not to consider what the end of my contract looks like. It's only just begun, and you're right, if we're meant to be, everything will work out exactly as it's supposed to."

Clutching the coffee in my hands, I take a much-needed hit of caffeine. "Jesus, I forgot how strong you love your coffee. I'm not sure why you bother to add milk at all."

Kassidy shrugs. "Figure you could do with the extra shot today. It looks like you barely slept last night."

"Yeah, it was almost daylight when we finally closed our eyes. Waking up to a wedding announcement isn't my idea of a lazy Sunday, though."

"May I ask..."

"What's the real story?"

"Yeah. Last night at the gala, Jarett asked if you two were dating. Gabe said yes, and you answered no, taking off like your dress was on fire."

Chuckling, I nod. "Gah. I wasn't prepared for the question, you know? I mean, after showing up to my birthday party together, I assumed it was self-explanatory. But when asked, I panicked. We never actually defined what we are. For all I know, he's seeing any number of women back in New York."

"You can get that theory out of your head immediately," Gabe's voice breaks over our conversation, not hearing him approach. "I haven't been on a date with any woman, other than you, since last year's gala."

Kassidy glances at me, her smile wide. I picture animated love hearts flashing in her pupils. "Aww, that's where you two met, right?"

Gabe acknowledges the fact with a single dip of his head, his eyes glued hard and fast to mine.

"Right, well, Jarett and I should get going and let you two figure some things out. Do you need anything before we leave?"

"Thanks, but..."

"I'll be here until tomorrow morning. If she needs anything, I'm good for it." There he goes again, taking charge and acting like I'm incapable of looking after myself.

Kassidy either doesn't notice or couldn't give a monkey's dick. She leans in to kiss me goodbye as Jarett joins us. "I take it we're heading off?"

"Yeah, we promised Roman we'd stop by to fill him in on everything after we saw you. He's worried but couldn't leave the café."

I nod, appreciating the sentiment.

Kassidy's glance bounces between Gabe and me, her body language suggesting she's bursting to divulge something but holding back. "What is it, Kassidy?"

Flicking her finger back and forth from her to Gabe, she says, "It's not going to be awkward? Us working together, I mean. With you two dating or *getting married*, me with Jarett…"

"Not weird unless you make it that way."

"Noted." She nods thoughtfully before wishing us good luck and allowing Gabe and me to finish our discussion.

Chapter 14

SOPHIA

"Marriage, Gabe?" I pace across my living room now we're free from visitors. It's early afternoon, and I'm on my second glass of wine. Gabe called down to the front desk earlier to confirm the paparazzi had finally cleared away from the front of the building.

"They put me on the spot, Sophia. I'm not going to apologize for it."

"I understand you thought you were doing the right thing, but a wedding?"

Anxiety pushes my feet faster around my apartment until the floor coverings are screaming at me to stop. Gabe is busy scrolling the internet, watching broadcasts and scanning the headlines.

"Stop. Please. Sit the fuck down."

The venom in his voice halts my flurry of steps. I

cross my arms and stare at Gabe, challenging him to order me to sit down once more.

"Pacing wildly around the room isn't helping anyone."

Nobody said it was but sitting won't make a world of difference either. Instead of pacing, I march into the kitchen and pour another glass of wine.

"They accosted me as I was returning to your apartment with two coffees in hand. When they accused you of sleeping with a client, I set them straight. I told them I've never been a client, and we were in a committed relationship."

Returning to the table where Gabe has now closed his laptop, I pull up a chair across from him.

"Wishful thinking on my part," he adds wryly.

And we're back to labeling our relationship. Engaged is where it's at now, apparently, but I remain silent and let him continue.

"The questions were flying and to shut it all down, I threw out the '*m*' word and walked away before the vultures wanted details I couldn't give."

Selfishly, I've been focused on the repercussions on myself and Incontro, yet Gabe has implicated himself more than he'd have liked to.

"I'm sorry, Gabe. I know this isn't what you want either."

With a shake of his head, he laughs. "You think I'm worried about having to pretend we're getting married? If it were true, I'd be ecstatic. It's knowing the idea has you doubled over in disgust that pisses me off."

"That's not true. I'm not disgusted by the thought. I'm worried about how we move forward from here in the eyes of the media. And I want to know who provided them with the incorrect information about you being a client of mine."

"Bad intel, a dodgy source, a jealous competitor… it could be any number of things. The most important thing is clearing your name and setting the record straight."

I nod slowly. "You're right. What's done is done, and we'll rise from this stronger than ever. Stacy is convinced we can turn this into a fairy-tale love affair of sorts." Internally, I cringe at the idea but refrain from letting Gabe know my true feelings on this.

"I have to fly back to New York tomorrow, and we need a game plan before I leave."

GABE

"It's not a question, Sophia. This is happening."

Her annoyance is evident, but after my public declaration of claiming her as my soon-to-be bride, what choice do I have?

At least that's what I tell myself.

"Another week and the press will have moved on to something more newsworthy. You moving to London is ridiculous."

Back in New York a few short days, and I already have the wheels in motion.

Imagining her feisty eyes and playfully pouty lips and the way my body responds to her is all I need to know that this is the right move.

"Despite your take on the situation, Sophia, I'll see you tomorrow. Goodnight, wife to be," I add as she huffs into the phone and hangs up.

Next on the agenda is to text Nigel to have him prepare the jet. I send a quick email to Elise to let her know of my plans. As we move closer to the new hotels and rebrand I hired Kassidy for, it makes perfect business sense to remain in London for the foreseeable future.

Whiskey in hand, I retreat to my Manhattan penthouse balcony with a cigar. Something about moving abroad brings back memories of my father. The only time I reach for a cigar is when I'm thinking of him.

Growing up, I'd watch him from a hidden corner in our living room in the evenings as he lit up and drowned his tears in a bottle of Jack. I knew of his pain but was at a loss as to what to do.

After my mother died when I was eight, once her body could no longer endure the stress of the chemotherapy and multiple rounds of radiation, my father worked less and drank like he'd once worked—with one hundred percent dedication and laser focus.

My mother was Italian, and her family all remained in Italy, so we had little in the way of family support. She met my dad while he was on vacation during a semester break at college and moved to the States within months to be with him. Less than a year later, they were married, and a few years later, I was born.

Dad's family disowned him for his relationship with my mother, a poor Italian woman barely old enough to fly across the country. They always saw my mother as a petty woman looking for a golden ticket to wealth and freedom.

By the age of nine, I became the proverbial parent to a broken-hearted drunk who could no longer pay his bills or put food on the table. They were the hardest years of my life. My mother was my world, and without her, I was lost.

Looking back now, I thank my father for the lessons he cast upon me.

The lack of security and the fear of not knowing where the next dollar for groceries would come from, made me the successful entrepreneur I am today.

During my early teenage years when dad passed out at night, I'd sneak into his study and read every piece of literature he kept hidden in there. I spent hours skimming through his emails, learning his way of doing business, creating relationships, and closing deals.

When we were a happy family of three, my father was a successful realtor. A man I looked up to. Now, I wouldn't spit on his grave if the devil breathed fire upon it.

That's why as far as Sophia is aware, I'm an orphan from Connecticut. It was easy to relate, knowing her parents passed when she was in her early twenties.

Almost at rock bottom, I returned home from school one day to find my father almost resembling his old self. He greeted me with a smile and the long-ago familiar spicy cologne wafted throughout the house, replacing the stench of cigar and whiskey.

"Hey, Son, how about we go out for a meal tonight?" I recall my confused expression making him laugh.

That evening, we ate at my favorite burger joint. Sauce dripped from the bottom of the bun all over my favorite Giants shirt, and Dad had laughed at my mortification.

"Soon, we'll be able to buy all the shirts you want, Son. In fact, we should buy season tickets to the Giant's home games."

Even at such a young age, I wasn't sure how this

would be possible. The week before, we'd been collecting pennies from between the cushions on the sofa to buy bread and milk. Eating out was a long way from that, and season tickets, they were for rich people. At that time, we couldn't have paid for the fuel to take the two-hour trip to New York.

Over the course of our meal together, my father explained a business deal he'd been offered. The details were vague, but he assured me it was the turning point. He was going to clean himself up, *execute the deal,* and the financial reward would change our lives. It was a happy moment for me when he promised to groom me in the real estate business so we could work together as partners when I was old enough.

He also told me I could choose any college I wanted to go to, and money would never be an issue again.

Later in life, I learned there was a lot of truth to these promises. Our lives changed, and money flooded in until he was torn away from me and locked in a high-security prison. Thankfully, by that stage, the business had been signed over to my father's attorney until I was of legal age to take charge. Financially, I was safe and secure.

As I learned the events that led to my father's incarceration, my idolized view of him lessoned to hatred and disgust. The company he'd left me to run alone was nothing more than the constant reminder of the monster my father had become.

My view of the entire world changed, and I no longer wanted to be associated with the Bartholomew name.

Lost in the view of the city lights and distant hum of busy traffic in the streets below, I allow myself a moment to wonder what he might think of me if he were alive today. Would he be proud of my achievements?

Did he regret his decisions that destroyed the only family I had left?

With blood on his hands, he destroyed more in that one shitty business deal than he ever realized.

Chapter 15

SOPHIA

Life isn't always unicorns and fairy dust. Occasionally, it throws in a tumble weed of what-the-fuck and makes you beg for mercy. This week has consisted of the latter, and my days of begging are numbered. Not twenty-four hours after my life was upended in the most public of ways, Gabe flew home to New York and left me to navigate the shitstorm he helped create.

Last night, he forcefully indicated he was moving to London so we *could be together.* Obviously, his intentions are to appease the press and have us appear to be in the committed relationship he so disrespectfully lied about.

The problem is, I despise the ideology that we should make more of our recurring casual flings to suit others. People-pleasing leaves a dirty taste in my mouth as does lying about my life.

Following the media massacre on Sunday after the gala, print stands all over the city are filled with more front-page news of our engagement and why I'm not wearing a ring with a diamond that screamed *owned by Gabe Lugreno*.

The pages that follow highlight my hard work and dedication to the sex trafficking cause and admirably, online donations are pouring in thick and fast. That's a unicorn I'm grateful for.

My work colleagues and long-standing clients are backing me with adoration after being served with papers from my legal team advising them to avoid making any statements or public announcements in relation to the matter.

Including Miguel Bishop. One of my elitist clients who propositioned me a few years ago.

The trouble with money-hungry media thugs?

They will scour the ends of the earth to find what they're looking for, and if it can't be found, they'll manufacture what's required to give them the byline.

After the positive story on page two of the Monday newspaper, there was a scandalous throwback to my evening with Miguel. However, the images supporting the story were from an event that took place two years after the fact. It was two colleagues discussing business over a drink, nothing more.

The worst scenario from this outrageous media blast is Miguel suing us for outing his membership to Incontro, declared to be a secret dating society for the elite. Of course, the fact Miguel used our services for prestige escorts on his visits to the Big Smoke rather than be paired with a suitor for a potential long-term committed relationship could've ended badly for us.

Despite our concerns, this scenario came out sprinkled with fairy dust. Miguel is openly a player in the socialite stratosphere and chose to use this media coverage of our explicitly incorrect affair for his benefit, which also benefited us. The request to decline to answer all media questions, which he blatantly ignored, turned in our favor.

"I could refuse to comment on this absurd accusation, however, let me take this opportunity to say I'm a huge fan of Sophia Evans as the personality behind Incontro and their services I highly recommend. As to the affair, I assure you, I have never been so lucky. Without a doubt, Sophia Evans doesn't operate her business in that manner. Believe me, I tried, but she shot me down in flames." He further directed women to reach out to him on Instagram for a code to subscribe to Incontro at a discounted rate.

All his doing, it was a positive show of support, though one which cast a shadow of doubt as to whether we set him up with his response and elaborately divulged this 'discounted membership scam' to hide the truth.

Which brings me to where I am today, having my hair and makeup done for an on-air interview with the British equivalent of *Ellen*, talk-show host, Desiree, in her celebrity hour segment.

"Who knew I'd make the celebrity hour once I hit forty," I cheer from my chair at the cosmetic station, highlighter and contouring being brushed over my face.

The makeup artist smiles politely but offers no response.

"Remember the lines, Sophia. That's all you need to do. This hour of fame could make or break you." Stacy, my publicist, has coached me through many situations in the past, but none where I'm the victim of lies that threaten to tear down the empire I've spent my life building and nurturing.

"I'm aware. But like I've said, I have nothing to hide."

"And everything to lose," Stacy warns.

Yeah, there's that.

I step from my throne in front of the mirror in the direction of the makeup assistant and follow the set director to backstage, where the filming is taking place.

Suddenly, the jacket I was forced to wear during the wardrobe stage of my morning begins to itch. Nerves rattle around in the pit of my stomach until a thin film of sweat covers my sweaty palms and traces back over my arms, my body heat mixing with the harsh fabric of the jacket causes a prickly feel. With moments left of the current segment, I shrug out of the jacket and make sure my girls are on full and even display in the sassy black dress Stacy insisted I wear.

"What are you doing? You're going live in less than three minutes," Stacy chastises.

"And I won't be doing it in that jacket unless you want me breaking out in hives on public television," I add, ignoring her advice from earlier to cover up and avoid sending an overtly sexy message to the audience. I promptly remind her I'm not on trial for prostitution.

Meh. I am who I am. If people are to believe what I say, they'll have a better chance when I present true to myself.

And by that, I mean, sexy, sassy, and vivacious.

The director cuts to an ad break as the audience cheers from their seats.

With the clock ticking, I run my hands down the length of my sleeveless, low-cut dress and take a deep breath, my eyes closing momentarily as I ready myself for what's ahead.

When they open, my gaze falls on the man set to turn my world upside down, in and out of the bedroom.

Gabe *fucking* Lugreno.

Chapter 16

SOPHIA

"You proactively stand against sexual harassment in the workplace. How do you expect people to believe your stance now you've been openly accused of sleeping with clients?" The question hits me where it hurts.

"Firstly, as I previously mentioned, every accusation recently printed is a blatant lie, and my legal team is taking action against the newspaper as we speak. Gabe and I have been dating for a year, we are engaged, and yes, we are sleeping together." The audience laughs, allowing me to take a pause and catch my breath.

"However, Gabe Lugreno isn't, and never has been, a client of Incontro or our sister agency, Heavenly Matches in New York. Therefore, my stance on sexual harassment has not changed, nor should it be viewed that way. I do and always will advocate for women *and men* who are victims of sexual harassment, sexual abuse, or sex trafficking."

"Is there anyone you're aware of who would take these unsubstantiated claims, as you put it, to the press, and furthermore, what reason would they have to slander your name like this?"

"This is a matter we're looking into. At this time, we have no information to share but believe me, my team and I *will* get to the bottom of this."

A sigh of relief escapes as I step down from the torturous line of questioning Desiree hit me with. The crowd is on their feet. Power to the women who take charge, own their beauty, their success, and don't apologize for who they are. That's what they're really saying as they clap their hands together as I leave the stage.

My first *live* on-air experience and I killed it. Kudos to Stacy for prepping me so well on every aspect of the interview. The audience appeared to be in favor of suing the newspaper for defamation, and I had no issue publicly broadcasting our intent to do so.

Incontro's legal team is tasked with serving the documents while I went live on national television. Apparently, suing an individual reporter for not giving up their source can be difficult to hold up in court, but not the newspaper responsible for printing the unsubstantiated lies. We have the money to run them out of the publishing industry for defaming a credible name and potentially ruining my livelihood.

"Gabe." I smile widely as I approach him, all eyes on us.

"Hello, sweetheart." He reaches for me and pulls me to him, briefly teasing me with his lips on mine.

"What are you doing here?" I whisper in his ear as I allow him to embrace me.

Being in his arms is hardly problematic, but it's often easier to pretend I don't want to be.

"Didn't want to miss the big moment." He grins, his gaze roaming the length of my neck and coming to a stop at my cleavage. "Let's get out of here."

"I have to go back to the office. My day isn't nearly over yet."

"I imagine after that scoop, your phones will be running off the hook with wannabe socialites and less than suitable escort applications."

"You have no idea." Since the report about Miguel surfaced, Incontro is the name on every woman's lips. Everyone wants a chance to date the elite bachelors of London. The problem is, until my team finishes damage control, and I've had a chance to personally speak with every client on our books, I'm unprepared to confirm we'll have need for more escorts.

If the male clients, many who are married and

looking for non-sexual dates for business meetings, can't trust me or the company with their information, they won't need our services any longer.

Taking my hand, Gabe walks me to his car out front of the studio. "Hop in, I'll drive you." He opens the door and ushers me inside.

"Hello, Miss Evans," Viktor welcomes me from the front seat. "Pleasure to see you again."

"Likewise, Viktor."

"I understand we'll be seeing much more of each other in the future." He winks, his bright smile lighting up the rearview mirror as Gabe settles into the seat beside me.

"I've heard the same rumor. You might be onto something there," I tease.

Gabe loosens his tie as if he's allergic to the proximity of his shirt collar around his neck.

"When did you arrive?" I ask, silently wishing I could play hooky and spend the rest of the day in bed with him.

"Earlier this morning, I had some things to take care of at the office before I came to you."

"You didn't have to. Be there, I mean."

"No, I didn't." He swivels in his seat to speak to me directly. "But that's how it's going to be moving forward."

His no-bullshit tone makes it difficult to argue, and honestly, it's the least of my concerns now.

"I was hoping you'd have some time early evening to look at some places I've picked out."

My eyebrows draw together in a frown. "You want me to look at investment properties with you?" This is all too much. On the verge of putting my foot in my mouth, Gabe chokes on a laugh.

"For an intelligent woman, you can be quite daft, you know?"

"Excuse me?" Straightening my back, I roll my shoulders, ready to give him a piece of my daft mind when he launches into a sales pitch about—

"Say again, you lost me." I zoned out as the blood rushed from my head to my toes.

The air surrounding us becomes heavy with animosity, and I clutch at my throat as if a tyrant has both hands clasped tightly around me, crushing my windpipe.

"Sophia, are you okay? You're sweating up a storm and lost all your color."

Nodding, I rummage through my handbag for my calming mist, something I use more for the scent than anything, though I'm in hell of a need of a sedative right now.

"I was saying, I've reserved a few times this evening to walk through a suite and penthouse loft, very close to where you are currently."

Right. "Wouldn't it be more practical to lease the suite you're currently in on a long-term basis?"

Gabe sits back, his eyes wide and searching my

face as if looking for flaws. He's shit out of luck there, it's one thing to enjoy thrift shopping at boutique galleries, but I've never skimped a penny on my skin care routine.

"You'd prefer to move into the Palace?"

"What? No. I love my apartment. I was thinking for you, save you the trouble of creating a new home. You've been staying in the same place ever since you started coming here."

The car pulls to the curb outside Incontro, and Gabe shakes his head, his lips twitching as he suppresses a smile. "Thank you for the lift," I offer as I step out of the vehicle, politely held open by Viktor. I straighten my dress and bend to see Gabe through the open window. "Will I see you tonight?"

"I'll meet you here at six."

Gliding through the front door as if I'd single-handedly taken down a lion, I'm met with a room full of staff and colleagues holding champagne glasses. "Congratulations!" they cheer as I meet their alliance with a shocked expression.

My love for these people is bountiful. "Did something happen?" I act as if I don't understand the cause for celebration. They wouldn't have it any other way. My colleagues know me better than anyone, even my family, and we're close.

Kelli laughs. "Boss lady, you killed it on the air today. Our online booking system has crashed three times since the interview ended. We have..."

she glances down at her iPad before continuing, "... over eighty new applications for socialites slash escorts, ten new applications for consultants, and fifty-two new elite membership requests."

If not for the cheering and clapping of hands, you could've heard my jaw drop to the floor. "That's more than our annual growth projections in less than..." I tap my phone to check the time, "... an hour. Holy shit."

Glancing around the room at my forty-four employees, if they're all in house, I do something I've never done before. "Go home. All of you." I wave my hand indifferently, and nobody dares to move. I'm met with deranged expressions, concern their fearless leader has lost her marbles.

"Unless you have clients to meet with, I suggest you move on out before I change my mind. Take the afternoon, spend some extra time shopping, take a train to the beach, enjoy your families if you have them. Fully paid."

Quiet murmurs start at the back of the group as some of them begin to stagger away from the group to gather their belongings.

"Kelli, can I see you before you leave, please?"

"Ah-ha." She gives me an animated nod as I walk to my office, ignoring those who aren't quite sure whether to take me seriously.

Once I'm alone with Kelli, I slump into the sofa with a bottle of red wine from my secret wine rack beneath my desk. "On it," she sings, detouring to the shelves where I keep the glasses and returns with one for each of us.

"Are you okay?"

Concern etches her voice as she overpours each of the glasses.

"A year and a few days ago, I sat in this same office pulling apart reasons to go to lunch with Gabe Lugreno after meeting him at the gala. If I had chosen not to go, none of this would be happening now."

A selfish thought and one I know to be useless and unproductive, but it's my thought all the same.

"It's not his fault, you know. Neither of you has done anything wrong. I don't think it would matter who you were dating. Some reporters desperate to make a wage will go to extraordinary lengths."

"Why are you so levelheaded about all this?" I sigh, wishing for once I had Kelli's outlook on life.

"We're in this together, Sophia. If it affects you, it affects me. I have no doubt you can handle this. Besides, your business is blowing up. It's everything you could've dreamed of."

Laughter bubbles within and escapes me, catching us both off guard. "Woman, that's the best pep talk you can come up with?" Kelli shrugs, and her giggle turns to full-blown laughter as we toast to the craziness that's my life in the limelight.

Fuck the media.

And fuck Gabe Lugreno.

"Gabe expects us to move in together," I say after we've fallen into a comfortable silence for a few minutes.

"Makes sense."

My head spins to the right, a frown cast over my brow. "Seriously? You too?"

Again, Kelli shrugs. "The declaration has been made, and he's committed to making it believable. Can't blame the guy."

"Hmm." I'm unsure what to say to this.

"I actually think it's a sweet gesture, Soph. He wants to do what's right for you and your reputation."

"You think I'm being too harsh on him?"

Kelli levels with me, meeting my eyes, "I think you're being too hard on yourself."

Chapter
17

SOPHIA

Taking Kelli's advice, I agree to meet with Gabe to look at the suites he arranged for us to view.

"Can you see yourself living here?" he asks as we take the elevator back down to the ground floor.

I'm hesitant to admit the top-level suite which expands the full floor overlooking the river, with the London Eye lit up in the distance, would be a perfect place to reside. The space is elegant and sophisticated, and with my personal touches, I'd be proud to call it home.

And the rooftop gardens with a three-hundred-and-sixty-degree view of London city are to die for.

But I love my apartment.

And my life.

Living it on my own terms without cause for question by any other person.

"You don't like it," he adds when my silence continues.

"It's not that, Gabe. Moving in together is a lot when it's only for a short time. Wouldn't it be easier to stage a break-up, let the media have their jilted bride story, and be done with it?"

Practicality wins, in my opinion. Moving out of my apartment, which I love immensely, and the time spent decorating a new residence to make it a home hardly seems worth it for the sake of appeasing people who mean nothing to either of us.

"You want to break up?" Gabe stops in his tracks after stepping out of the elevator and turns to me. "Is that honestly the way you want to play this?"

With a sigh, I lift my eyes to his and falter at the emotion I see looking back at me. "Were we ever really together?" I whisper quietly.

"Fucking hell, Sophia, how can you ask me that? You don't honestly believe I have this much work to attend to out of our London office, do you? I travel here mostly to spend time with you. I haven't thought of another woman since we met."

"You haven't?"

Honestly, other men are far from my mind, too, but it's not a conscious decision. I simply have no interest. Besides, Gabe takes care of all my needs in every way a man should.

"We never talked about being exclusive," I continue defensively.

"My wanting to tell your brothers about us wasn't enough of a clue?" The foolish look on his face, eyebrows raised, I can't help but laugh at him. Yet, I'm the one who should be laughed at.

"And I shut you down without a second thought."

He takes my hands in his, caressing my knuckles with each of his thumbs. "Yeah, about that. I may have told them at the gala that I intended to make you mine."

"You did?" My eyes widen at his admission, and my pulse raises a few beats per minute.

"Fuck woman, you amaze me. You're so wrapped up in your clients finding love, you're blinded to the idea for yourself. I intend to change that. But for now, let's head back to your place, and I'll remind you what you'd be missing by denying me."

"Now that's a challenge I'm willing to accept."

"There was no doubt in my mind."

GABE

We barely make it through the door at Sophia's with our clothes on. She escapes my grasp to dump her briefcase and handbag on the table, and I'm not a fan of waiting. They weren't handing out patience the day I was born.

From behind, I lift her blouse, and my hands

123

sneak below the waistband of her pants. "Ohh." She leans back into my chest as I rub her clit with the tip of my finger, desperate to seek out her wet pussy.

Seconds later, I'm done with the fabric between us. Tugging Sophia's pants down swiftly, I then strip her shirt off and spin her toward me. I make quick work of removing her bra and panties and cover her nipples with hot kisses. She loves when I scrape my teeth over the hardened tips, and I can't resist.

Maybe it's the idea of moving in with her or marrying her, I don't know, but I'm as horny as a teenager watching his first porno. I position Sophia on the table's edge in front of me, and she quickly helps me out of my shirt. As soon as I have her resting on the table, propped up on her outstretched hands, she lifts her legs over my shoulders and I unbuckle my pants, promptly stepping out of them when they fall to my feet.

Not wanting to waste any time, I dive between her thighs, missing the taste of her something fierce. Her sweet arousal is my drug of choice, and I can't live without it. The idea is maddening. I feast on her pussy until she's squirming out of my hold, her thighs shaking uncontrollably, and her juices dripping from my chin.

"I need your cock, Gabe."

"Tell me you miss it," I growl, needing to hear the words.

"I miss it as much as you miss my pussy, now, fuck me. Please."

My cock is so hard, it fucking hurts. Entering her, it takes all my control not to come on the first stroke. Minutes later, I can't be bothered holding back any longer. With every thrust into her wetness, I watch her breasts bounce from the movement and tease her clit with my fingers until she's screaming at me for a release.

"Gabe, I need to come. Please, Gabe, please…"

As I lean over her slightly, I see the moment I hit her sweet spot. When I feel her walls squeeze my cock, I'm a goner. "Come, sweetheart, let it go."

Our breaths come out heavy and loud as we succumb to the ecstasy that keeps bringing us back together.

When we finally move, I help Sophia to the floor, and collect her clothes. I chuckle when I glance at the table. "Maybe we'll eat on the sofa tonight?"

Chapter 18

GABE

After I attend to some early morning work calls, I leave Sophia's place to return to my suite and prepare for the day ahead. First up, I have a meeting with Kassidy about the next steps in our hotel design project. Hiring her is the best thing I've ever done despite the tension it has caused between Jarett and myself.

Unfortunately, the tension only grew when he found out I was sleeping with his sister. Though it wasn't my intention to keep it a secret from him, it was also not my place to announce it. That was Sophia's call, and as much as her opposing to do so drove me wild, I had to respect it.

Especially since I never exactly divulged I knew Jarett.

Following the meeting with Kassidy, we're both

due to meet with Markus Walton, the owner of the new hotel chain. It's an informal meet and greet as we haven't fully commenced work on the project, but while he's visiting for other reasons and I'm also in town, inevitably, it's a great opportunity for him and Kassidy to meet face to face.

Once all the meetings and work commitments are out of the way, I focus on the real reason I'm in London and prepare to make a home I am happy to spend my time in away from the office.

With Sophia.

"Gail, Gabe Lugreno. You can expect to receive an offer any minute from my lawyer for the Sky suite my fiancé and I viewed yesterday."

"Yes, Mr. Lugreno. I have your offer in front of me. It's above the asking price, you realize?"

"I'm aware, yes. You said it was move-in ready. I can transfer the funds immediately and pick up the key this afternoon if possible?"

"Oh, umm, these transactions don't usually move ahead this quickly, sir, although the seller has agreed to the terms and price in your paperwork."

Of course, they have. And I knew she'd have sent them the offer already. My team emailed and called her office an hour ago after already discussing with the owner.

I have an appointment with an interior designer in two hours and furniture due to be delivered in less than an hour. I'm not one to fuck around when

I know what I want. Sophia will forgive me when I explain the plans for her apartment in Shoreditch.

"I'll have my attorney transfer the funds immediately, and I'll be right over to sign the final paperwork and accept my keys. Thank you, Gail. It's been a pleasure."

Without waiting for her answer, I hang up the phone and transfer the funds. I don't actually need my attorney, Brad, to take care of this part of the transaction for me.

SOPHIA

The best start to the day is reading the retraction in today's news, together with the public apology slandering my name. Well, except for hot and sweaty morning sex with the man who's committed to taking over my life.

With all the team back on board after their early send-off yesterday, we gather in the boardroom to celebrate the news and rehash the policies surrounding staff relationships with clients, just in case there's any question of where I stand on this.

We still haven't uncovered the source of the misinformation or the reason behind it, but we will. I have sources I'm hoping will talk more freely now the retraction has been printed.

While my staff is aware Gabe has never been a

client of Incontro, I don't want there to be any misunderstanding. The staff from our New York agency are also present via video conference, so I take this opportunity to address the introduction to the elite membership side of our international counterpart. Bree and I have already discussed this and agree now's the time to put our best foot forward and start to turn the tide on that extension of our business.

"As you all know, during my regular trips to New York over the past year, I have been training consultants in the management of our elite membership base and services. While our sister agency to date has remained focused on their original matchmaking services alone, we feel now is the best time to move forward with the introduction of our high-end escort services."

A round of applause fills the room. It's a big step for all involved. I've assigned my top London consultants to partner with my pick of those in New York to mentor and assist with providing the best support in this area. Our clientele pays us a huge sum to vet their potential dates for suitability and trust their role isn't to be taken lightly.

"We'll be rolling this out with the help of our media and web development team over the weekend. Media coverage commences tomorrow with the exclusive membership portal launching on Saturday. This won't affect most of you, but for our senior consultants assigned to a member of our team in New York, please be prepared to assist where needed. You'll be required to be on call over this weekend to answer any questions as previously discussed."

It's been almost a year since we purchased the international agency, and slowly we've been changing the brand and reconditioning the expectations of the current clientele. Also, a great deal of time has been spent engaging potential new client interest to assist with the success of this launch. New York is highly competitive regarding their elite services for high-rollers and secret society members, so it's definitely not without its challenges, though each challenge is worth tackling head- on.

"Did you and Gabe pick a new place to call home last night?" Kelli whispers as we leave the conference room after a brief Q and A.

"Not exactly. I'm still not convinced me uprooting my apartment to move in with him *for show* is worth it." Plus, we didn't discuss it any further after we returned to my place, but I wasn't about to tell her the reason for that.

"You won't know until you try." Kelli's cheery positivity about my current situation both irritates me and puts a smile on my face at the same time.

Part of me believes there's nothing to lose. The other churns in contempt at having to share a space with another human. I'm forty, for fuck's sake, and have been living alone for half of my life. I love my privacy and not having to answer to anyone.

And I know Gabe is unprepared for the hundreds of pairs of shoes I own.

To my knowledge, he's never had a relationship serious enough to share a home with a woman before me, and it's a recipe for disaster.

"I'll be heading out by five this afternoon. I think Mr. Lugreno and I have some serious discussing to do."

"Would you like me to type out your pros and cons list to take with you?" she asks, grinning from ear to ear.

"What list?" I snap, forgetting she knows me better than I know myself most of the time.

"The one in the top drawer of your desk…" she laughs, "… where you keep all your lists for the important stuff."

I march off to my office, leaving her in a fit of giggles.

Bitch.

When I finish up a few hours later after an in-office meeting with yet another unsuitable applicant, I pull my hardcover notebook from my drawer and open to my current list of pros and cons. Yes, Kelli was right. What she doesn't know is there's only one entry on the pros side of the list.

Hot sex on tap.

Although we planned to meet for dinner at eight, I decide to head home early to recharge, change, and study the apartment I love so dearly. It's a chance to reflect and try to imagine my life and home being uprooted and moved to the Sky suite, my favorite choice from the two suites we viewed last night.

Entering my building, Ray greets me with a confused look from the reception desk. "Hello, Miss Evans, did you forget something?"

"I'm sorry?" I ask, unsure why he'd assume I'd forgotten something as it has been ten hours since I left for work this morning.

Ray's smile broadens, "Don't tell me Mr. Lugreno failed to deliver part of your monstrous shoe collection."

Frowning, I walk to the desk where Ray sits. He's worked here for several years now. The day the laborers arrived to remodel part of my closet to make room for my collection, he was new to the position.

"What was Mr. Lugreno doing with my shoes, Ray?"

Horror fills his eyes, his smile drops, and he begins to stammer. "You... you don't know?" he finally whispers.

Dread wafts over me, and my body stiffens. My throat seizes as if I've scooped a little too much Chunky Monkey ice cream into my mouth and tried to swallow it without chewing.

"Know *what*?"

"Perhaps you should call Mr. Lugreno yourself." His beady little eyes dance around, avoiding direct contact with mine.

Pulling my phone from my bag, I powerwalk to the elevator and swipe my access card. The call goes straight to voicemail, and I let out an exasperated huff as I punch the keys to my floor in the elevator.

Now, my blood is coursing angrily through my veins, and I see red. Eager to get into my apartment, I trip over the lip of the elevator, my heel getting stuck in the gap.

"Fuck," I curse loudly as I fall forward, dropping my briefcase and... *snap.*

There goes the heel on my favorite Friday Louis Vuittons.

Picking myself up off the floor, I step out of my shoes so I don't go ass up again and eventually make my way into my apartment.

"The fuck?" I yell, spinning around my once vibrantly decorated apartment, finding nothing but open space.

Everything is gone.

Chapter 19

GABE

After my last call for the evening ended, I notice several missed calls from Sophia. Glancing at the time, she shouldn't be finished with work yet. We're supposed to be meeting for dinner in fifteen minutes.

Fuck.

Being late is for people with no drive and nothing to lose. Tonight, isn't the night to show up late. I call Viktor to have him swing around front to pick me up. As I race to meet the car, I return Sophia's call and curse when she doesn't answer.

Running through the notifications and messages on my phone, I stop when I see Sophia's name. I open the alert as I step off the elevator, and hurricane Sophia rushes me. Wild, disheveled, and ready to stake me in the heart with her acrylic fingernails, I step back with my hands in the air.

She knows.

My heart sinks momentarily. This isn't how I wanted her to find out.

"You outrageously pompous, arrogant fucktard! You moved me out of my apartment?"

Hesitantly, I remind her, "We spoke about this."

"No, you spoke about it. I recommended a very public breakup and told you how much I loved my apartment." She stabs me in the chest and clutches her hand in pain.

"Motherfucker."

Amused, I watch as she dances on the spot, her rage replaced with the pain of jarring her nail on my abs. I'd say I'm sorry, but I can't risk laughing.

"If it makes you feel any better, I handled your shoe collection myself?"

"Ugh. How could you?"

"Fuck me, Sophia. Why do you keep challenging me?"

She glares at me, her narrowed eyes full of contempt.

"Why do you keep pushing for us to do this?"

"Because I fucking love you, okay? *Fuck.*" The truth spills from my lips without consideration for the tone of delivery. And I instantly regret it.

Since my mother, I haven't said those words to any woman, and the emotion almost cripples me.

"You... you love me?" she whispers, tears

135

gathering in her eyes.

I pull her into a hug, and wrap my arms tightly around her, wishing I could take back the words. Tell her when the timing is better, like when we weren't in a heated argument, and she didn't want to stab me.

"You weren't supposed to find out this way. About the apartment or the way I feel about you."

She clutches my back, clinging to me as if she never wants to let me go.

I can only hope one day this will be true.

Because as much as she sees this as minimizing a media scandal, I see this as our opportunity at a life of love, filled with happiness and shared success neither of us has been privy to before.

"Viktor is waiting outside for us. Can we still make our reservation and discuss the details?"

Sophia steps back and lifts her eyes to mine.

"What choice do I have? You moved my life into a suite I don't have access to." Halfheartedly, she chuckles, and I pull an access card from my pocket and hand it to her.

"Now you do."

As we walk to meet Viktor patiently waiting for us, she adds, "I had to stop by the office after visiting my empty apartment to fetch a spare pair of heels after snapping a heel on my favorites. You better have my shoes perfectly displayed when I get home."

A grin the size of the Grand Canyon covers my face at her mention of *home.*

"If they're not to your standards, you can take it out on me in bed."

Laughing, she agrees. "Deal."

Dinner tonight is more about the conversation than wining and dining a woman into bed. With the knowledge I'll be waking up beside Sophia each morning for the foreseeable future makes me a privileged and happy man.

"What am I going to tell my brothers? Jesus, I haven't even discussed any of this with anyone besides Kelli."

"Why do you seek their approval?"

"It's not about their approval. They're my people, and their support means the world to me."

"And if they don't support you?"

"They will because they love me. It doesn't mean they'll agree with my choices, but they'll have my back whatever I decide to do. That's what family does."

The mention of family disarms me, and I bow my head to hide my emotion.

"Gabe." She reaches across the table and clutches my hand. "You've met all my family now, and you know about my parents. Now we're going to be *living* together, don't you think it's time to share with me?"

I know she's right. And she deserves all the

details, but some I'll never be able to fully disclose.

"What do you want to know?"

She pulls back from me with a quizzical expression. Granted, each time she's asked a personal question in the past year, I've clamped up like a soggy book—the pages glued together, afraid to open in the presence of someone who may see straight through their damaged center.

"You've shared briefly about your mother but never mentioned your father."

I reach for my whiskey to disguise my discomfort.

Ask about anything but my father, I want to tell her.

"I never knew him."

Mentally, I clout myself around the head. I have no idea why I lied. There's a difference between a straight-out lie and not disclosing the full truth, although both are shitty options.

"I'm so sorry."

"No. Stop." I push away from the table and bury my hands in my head. When I glance back at Sophia, her glare is a mix of emotions. I rake my fingers through my hair and start again.

"I don't know why I said that. My father died in my teens, he turned into a drunk after my mother died, and I prefer not thinking about him." I choke back the words I'll never be able to share with her.

"Siblings?"

Grateful for her moving on so quickly, I still can't offer any happier news.

"Only child." I smile. "I always wanted a sibling. It was lonely at times, especially after my mom passed."

"You said you grew up in Connecticut, so how did you end up in New York?"

"After both my parents..." I pause, "... after they died, and I was old enough to get the hell out of the area, I did and pursued my dreams at Columbia."

"Did you go into the foster care system after your father passed?"

I shook my head. "No, a group home for boys. Nobody wanted to foster a broken teenager."

Sophia considers my answer for a moment before giving up on the inquisition and taking a sip of her wine.

"Enough about family for one evening. Let's talk about our plan moving forward."

"Okay, tell me what you've done with my apartment." The tone of my words could tear a boulder to threads.

"I moved your belongings, Sophia, nothing more. Though I do have an idea for the apartment I think you'll love. But first, we should set a date for the wedding and make a public announcement."

"You know I'm not actually going to marry you, right? If I get married, I want it to be once only, not some ruse for the satisfaction of the media grubs."

She might think this way now, but I'll be fucked if I let her get away without making her mine forever. This woman has destroyed me for any other. She just doesn't know it yet.

Rising from the table, I take a small velvet box from inside my jacket. I've been carrying it with me since I arrived back in London, waiting for the right time.

Tonight, we'll go home to *our* place, and I can't think of a better time to make this official.

Rounding the table, I kneel on one knee at Sophia's side and take her hand.

She gasps and glances around the restaurant. Silence falls over the diners, and I feel their eyes are on us. Mine never leave hers.

"You've already said yes, but I wanted to do this properly with a ring this time."

It had to be said in case anyone was filming. The last thing we need is the media assuming my talk of marriage was an after-thought to the publication mess.

"Sophia, I've never met anyone like you. You're charismatic, bossy, you keep me on my toes, challenge me constantly, and you're beautiful, inside and out. Please make me the happiest man on earth and commit to me forever."

Her free hand flies over her mouth, and tears fill her eyes.

"Sophia, will you marry me?"

With the ring between my fingers, I begin to slip it over the end of her wedding ring finger. Waiting on bated breath for her answer before I set it in place. Come on, baby, say yes.

Please.

"Of course, Gabe. Yes, I'll marry you."

I glide the ring down her finger and it's a perfect fit. She admires the two-carat diamond encased in smaller ones before pulling me to my feet and launching herself into my arms.

The crowded restaurant erupts, clapping and shouting their congratulations, but I only have eyes for Sophia. With my hands on either side of her face, I crash my lips to hers and kiss her in a way I never have before.

With complete ownership.

She's mine.

And I vow to show her exactly what she'll be missing if she decides to leave.

Chapter 20

SOPHIA

"Sophia, what the fuck is going on?" Jarett yells through the phone.

Shit.

What time is it?

I wipe the sleep from my eyes as I roll out of bed. The room is still dark, and Gabe stirs as I try to compose my thoughts.

"Why aren't you answering your door?"

I intended to call Jarett and Roman once we arrived home from dinner last night, except Gabe made me a slave to his body until the early hours of this morning when we finally passed out.

"I'm not at my apartment."

I haven't even mentioned Gabe is back in town yet.

"Where the hell are you? Your so-called

My Billionaire Fling

engagement video is all over the fucking internet."

Fuckity fuck.

Oh yeah, about that.

"I guess I have some news to share with you all, but I need to get ready for work. We'll fill you in on everything tonight at Maximum."

"We? You're bringing Gabe to our family catch-up?"

"Seriously, Jarett. You're bringing Kassidy, yes?"

"That's different. I love Kassidy. And so do you!"

"And I lo... like Gabe." Glancing behind me, I know Gabe is pretending to be asleep, and I feel like an ass. Storming to the kitchen to brew some coffee, I whisper, "I love my reputation and my company, Jarett."

Exasperated, Jarett continues, "I know, Soph. But Saturday, you denied dating the guy, Sunday he declares to the world that you're getting married, and three days later, there's a live video with over two million views on the web of him proposing to you in public. And again, we're the last to know anything. Kassidy says you've not even mentioned anything to her, and a week ago, you two were joined at the hip."

"Okay, I get it. It's been a crazy few days. Things are happening faster than I'm able to keep up with, and frankly, my main concern is clearing my name in the media. But I do feel terrible that I've not kept you all in the loop. I'm sorry."

I have some serious groveling to do, starting with a call to Kassidy.

"I'll see you tonight and promise to tell you everything."

"Seems like tonight will be full of important announcements."

I place the milk on the counter and stop what I'm doing. "What do you mean?"

"You didn't get the group message from Roman last night?"

Gah. No. "Sorry, I was a little preoccupied celebrating my engagement," I add dryly.

"Please, spare me the details. Roman wants to discuss something with us tonight. No idea what but he said he has some happy news to share."

"Ooh, I wonder what it could be. I'll see you tonight, J."

Gabe sneaks up behind me as I'm pouring the coffee. "I guess we should've announced it to your family earlier?"

As I turn to face him, I whimper at the sight of the toned naked man who has me trapped in his arms. "Yes, but you can make it up to them tonight. You're coming to Maximum with me."

He trails wet kisses up the side of my neck, eliciting a moan. "Wouldn't dream of missing it."

Before I end up back in bed with him, I escape his classic morning seduction routine and take my coffee. After I slip out onto the terrace, I tie my robe at the waist.

It's strange waking up with his ring on my finger. Our nights spent together in New York and Paris were vastly different than they are now. Jarett's right, it's only been a matter of days, and we've moved from a secret fling to a public engagement.

My body shudders at the thought of what today's news will entail.

I open my phone, and dial Kassidy's number.

"Hello, stranger," she answers after the third ring, raising my guilt level by another bar.

"Don't you start. My brother is already pissed at me."

"Nah, he's hurt that you didn't involve him. He'll be fine. Me, though, I don't accept not having all the details." I've missed Kassidy's laugh. From the moment I met her, I'm pretty sure I fell in love with her as quickly as Jarett did. When I begged her to stay an extra week to be at my fortieth, I never could've imagined she'd remain here for a year.

Surprised doesn't even begin to cover my reaction when the revelation hit that my sexy younger man fling was the man who offered her a position and was the reason for her staying. Kassidy and Jarett are perfect together, and I couldn't be happier for them both.

If only Jarett can find it in his heart to show me the same support with Gabe.

"And I don't mean the details you'll be willing to

share tonight with your brothers present," she adds, bringing me back to the present.

"Like you openly told me about you and Jarett, you mean?"

"He's your brother, did you really want the ins and outs of our time together?"

Negative.

"Okay, you win. Of course not. But Gabe is your boss, so…"

"Fine. Keep your lips sealed. I don't want to imagine him naked when I see him next."

I laugh hard. "I promise you he's picture-perfect in all the right places."

"Enough!" Kassidy groans. "Forget I mentioned it."

"You know, if you'd told him about the two of you before your birthday, his reaction would've been extremely different."

"Agreed." I sigh as Gabe relaxes onto the lounger next to me. "Gabe suggested we tell them before the party, but I was stubborn. We weren't exactly dating, so I didn't see the point."

We lived in separate cities and hooked up when he visited. It hardly seemed like I needed to expose my sex life to them.

"Perhaps Gabe suggested this because he knew Jarett."

"Something I wasn't aware of until that night either."

"Yes, I know that, but does Jarett?"

God, what a clusterfuck. Could this world get any smaller?

"You're right. I'll clear that up with him." With a glance over at Gabe, I realize it's not a conversation we ever got around to having.

"Great, see you tonight. Oh, and happy engagement."

Chuckling, I thank her and end the call.

Gabe is staring at me when I place the phone beside me and caffeinate.

"Kassidy raised a valid point, you know."

"And what's that?"

"You were insistent about meeting Jarett and Roman before my birthday, and you know, telling them about us."

"If I remember correctly, you refused to acknowledge we were anything more than a casual fuck. Your words, not mine."

I choose to ignore him, and ask the question I should've wanted the answer to in the beginning. "You knew Jarett was my brother and you were in business together. Why didn't you tell me?"

What was the point of keeping it a secret?

It's hard to keep my head out of the gutter when he stretches his legs the full length of the lounge, and his nakedness is shielded only be a pair of boxer shorts.

"It wasn't my place to mention our relationship

147

to Jarett. And as you reminded me, our idea of the relationship was varied. I wanted to have the conversation before the party because of my business relationship with Jarett. I should've told you, but I didn't think it mattered to you if I knew him or not."

Silently, I accept his answer.

It wouldn't have made any difference to me if I knew.

But in hindsight, Jarett wouldn't have felt out of place or on edge about us if it hadn't come as such a shock to him. Granted, he learned of us at the same time he realized Kassidy's new boss was also the man on my arm. I understand how he may have felt a little blindsided by it all.

Gabe's phone blares to life, and I instantly recognize his dreamy voice from last night. "Let me see," I tell him, moving to crouch down beside him to view our viral engagement ruse.

Wow.

Emotions bubble in my chest as I watch both of us at that moment. I look so *happy*. Even knowing the proposal wasn't real, there isn't a doubt in my mind we appear one hundred and fifty percent in love and committed to each other.

My gaze wanders to Gabe, who's watching me intently, a warmth in his eyes I've only seen a few times. "We look great together, don't you think?"

To suppress my tears, I fake a cough and lean in

to kiss him. But one kiss isn't enough. I crawl over him until I'm sitting in his lap, my fingers tracing his abs as I devour his lips, and I tease him with my tongue until we're both moaning and I feel Gabe rising to attention beneath me. Tenderly, he brushes my morning hair behind my ears and cups my head in his hands as he explores my coffee-flavored mouth.

"I love you, Sophia."

His words whispered into our kiss threaten every defensive wall I've ever built around my heart to come crumbling down.

"Gabe," I whisper roughly.

"Shh, don't say anything. Just make love to me on the terrace. Right here, right now."

He doesn't have to ask me twice.

Chapter 21

SOPHIA

If every morning of married life begins the way it did today, call me married as fuck.

Bring on the wedding day already.

Except, happiness can't be promised from one day to the next, no more than life itself.

Growing up, I'd lay awake and listen to my parents argue in the library downstairs. They thought they were being discreet, keeping their arguments behind closed doors, but I saw what it did to them. The more Dad's oil business grew, the longer he spent on trips away and the less he and Mom enjoyed valuable time together.

The weekend of the accident, my father had arranged to travel to Texas to secure the biggest deal of his life. My mother begged him not to go. Unable to explain why, I recall her repeatedly saying she had a bad feeling about the affiliation.

In the end, Dad convinced Mom to go with him, promising her ten days traveling through Louisiana, Mississippi, and into Florida and down to the Keys once the deal was finalized. She'd always wanted to visit the south, and Florida was on her bucket list. It was the perfect opportunity for her to fulfill a dream and for them to spend some much-needed quality time together.

Except they never made it.

The light plane they traveled in from Fort Worth only made it halfway to the oil site before falling from the sky in a fiery ball of death, claiming the lives of my parents and the pilot.

My phone ringing breaks through my thoughts, and I'm pleased to see Kelli's face flashing on my screen. Tapping to answer, she greets me first. "You said yes!"

Holding the phone away from my ear, I wait until she calms down. She knows as well as I do it's all a sham but from day one, she's been team Gabe.

"Congratulations, you dirty whore," she blasts, "I'm so freaking happy for you. Tell me you watched the video this morning. God, you look so fucking happy. When did that happen?"

Ugh. Exactly what I didn't need. Confirmation of my thoughts from earlier.

"Last night at dinner," I say, knowing that's not what she's asking.

I cut her off. "I'll be in the office in five... hold your thoughts until then."

Eager to find some status quo in my day, I hang up.

As I round the corner in the direction of Incontro, I notice a swarm of reporters waiting by the door on the street.

Great.

Quickly, I escape into the nearest coffee shop, I call Stacy. "Sophia, I was just about to call you. The press is outside with cameras rolling, waiting for your arrival."

"I just saw them. I snuck into Wade's Coffee Shop to avoid them and call you. What's the plan? I take it you've seen the proposal this morning?"

"I have, and well done. World-class acting from both of you. Nobody will ever assume it's not true love."

Yeah, so I've heard.

"They'll want a close-up of the ring, a photo of the happy bride-to-be, and a date. Pluck one out of thin air if you haven't discussed this yet. Make it at least twelve months into the future so they won't be hounding you daily for new updates on wedding plans."

Okay. Sucking in a deep breath, I make my way to the office. Annoyed we didn't set a fake date when we spoke of it last night, I'll to have to wing it. We knew this would be the question on everyone's lips today.

Reporters swarm me as I approach, and I offer a radiant smile. Purposely, I flash my bling in their direction with a not-so-subtle flick of the hand. In this moment, I'm surprised how much I love the spotlight.

My ears ring with the best wishes and congratulations of people who honestly couldn't give a fuck. I play the game and give them what they need as questions begin flying.

"When's the big day?"

"Have you set a date?"

Waving my hands in the air to silence the herd, I give them the answer they want the most and try to slip inside. "We've decided on a long engagement, September 8th next year."

"Why so long?"

"How long have you been dating?"

The questions keep firing, many of the same asked in various ways, each reporter hoping for the scoop to satisfy their editors and engage their readers.

"Do you know the *real* Gabe Lugreno?"

Now that's a question I'm incapable of answering. My gaze bounces from face to face in front of me, searching for the reporter who posed the question. It isn't difficult as the crowd quietens down and all eyes turn to a man at the back. He appears to be in his late twenties, possibly early thirties, his expression eerily solemn and his dark eyes piercing mine.

Not the reporter type.

"That will be all for today, thank you."

Barreling through the door, I take a deep breath. *What the fuck was that?*

"Kelli, if they haven't left the premise within fifteen minutes, please call security to have them removed."

"Sure thing. Are you okay? You look beaten to a pulp."

I glance back outside and see the same man standing, hands deep in his pockets, staring at me with a peculiar grin through the glass door.

Without taking my eyes off him, I speak to Kelli. "The man staring in the jeans and black tee…" I wait for Kelli to acknowledge who I'm speaking of, "… get me a name and find out who he answers to, please."

Pushing my way through the team who have left their posts to see what all the commotion is about, I accept each of their congratulations with a gracious smile before I lock myself in my office.

I consider texting Gabe about the reporter's comments, but it was too vague of a question to cause concern for both of us. I opt to dig a little deeper myself before I share anything with Gabe, and that's when it hits me.

His accent. The mysterious man outside is an American.

Rushing to the front door, I find him, and the rest of the crowd has already moved on.

Dammit.

When I spin on my heels to return to my office, Kelli is sitting at her desk staring at me with a huge smile on her face.

"What's the ridiculous smile for?"

She pushes her chair back and saunters toward me.

"I'll get you the information you need in a few moments, but I'm dying to see."

My mind is scattered, and it takes a moment for me to understand why she's so deliriously happy and inquisitive.

"Show me the bling, baby," she sings, taking my hand and falling instantly in love.

"Holy shite, that's some serious diamond heist, Soph."

Squealing, she throws her arms around me, and I struggle to keep my feet on the ground enough to fold us both upright. A flutter of guilt lodges in my chest. I walked into the office throwing demands at her without so much as a hello, allowing her no chance to shower me with congratulations.

"I'm so excited for you," she carries on happily.

Smiling brightly, I thank her. "I know you are. But remember—"

"Yes, *I know*, but don't be a downer. When are we having a girl's night to celebrate?"

"This Saturday," I answer immediately, "Why the fuck not?" I'll let Kassidy and Maxine know tonight, and I'll make a call now to Jules, Holly, Karyn, and Bel to give them the news before they too see it on the web and come after me with pitch forks.

With Bel's hubby an editor-in-chief at a local women's magazine, I can only tell them what we need the world to believe. It's a good thing my acting skills are top-notch.

GABE

"Hey buddy, it's Ben."

"Miss me already?" I laugh.

"Somebody does, that's why I'm calling."

Instantly frowning, I take a seat at my desk and put my feet up.

"Go on."

"There was a guy snooping around here the other day, asking questions about you and how we know each other. Said he was an old friend."

"Did he give you a name?"

"Nah, man, said he hasn't seen you since you were young kids in Connecticut, and you probably wouldn't remember him anyways. Didn't think too much of it, but it got me thinking, you said you grew up in Jersey."

Running my fingers through my two-day-old growth, I contemplate what this means.

"Yeah, probably some money-hungry grub, looking for his five minutes of fame."

"I saw your woman on television just now, held up by the press outside her offices. The guy that was asking questions, he was there. I'm sure it was him."

Blood runs cold through my veins.

Once I say goodbye to Ben and thank him for the heads-up, I call Ronnie, my private investigator. He worked the case against my father, and in the end, it was his evidence that convicted him. Ever since, it's him I call if a matter requires investigation.

While I wait for him to answer, I search Google for the news broadcast Ben mentioned. There are no familiar faces in the crowd, but that doesn't mean anything.

"Ronnie, it's Gabe Lugreno. Call me as soon as you can on this number. I'm in London."

Sending him a quick email, I let him know I have a job for him, one I need carried out discreetly.

While I watch the brief interview of Sophia, I learn we have until September 8th next year to plan her perfect wedding. First, I need to up my game and convince her I'm the man she should marry.

For real.

Chapter 22

SOPHIA

Gabe arrives with a minute to spare. He hates tardiness, and I was beginning to think he'd forgotten.

"Can we have a minute to talk before we go in?"

"What's the matter?" I don't like the expression on Gabe's face. "Is it the wedding date? You saw the news report, I assume."

He takes my hand, shaking his head. "The date is perfect. Figure it gives me enough time to make you fall in love with me."

I chuckle. "You do, do you?"

His mood lightens, and I tuck my arm in his. "Whatever you need to discuss, can it wait? We really should get inside and face the questions."

Groaning, he says, "Something tells me their

questions will far outweigh those of nosey reporters."

You got that right, Mr. Lugreno. Buckle up for the onslaught.

The last time Gabe and I descended the stairs at Maximum, it was my fortieth birthday. I was dressed in a slutty corset, and Gabe wore a gangster suit and fedora hat. The reception we received from my family was less than inviting, and it had nothing to do with my barely-there choice of costume. It had everything to do with the man on my arm.

The same man I'm now engaged to for all intents and purposes.

A man who declared his love for me and willingly uprooted his life to protect me and my reputation.

At what point will I allow myself to give in to his pull over my heart?

"Ahh, here's the happy couple." Kassidy grins, leaving the booth to greet us both with a kiss.

"It's okay if I kiss you, right? I mean, we're practically family now." She taps Gabe playfully on the shoulder, and I'm grateful to her for lightening the mood.

Maxine is carrying a tray of drinks to customers in the booth behind ours, and greets us with a passing wink. "Congrats to the happy couple. Drinks are on the house tonight."

I love the women in my life, they make up for the stubborn testosterone shared by my brothers.

"Thanks, Max."

"So far, so good," Gabe whispers, adjusting his tie and taking the first step toward Roman and Jarett. Both of them remain seated in the booth with expectant expressions. I stare daggers at each of them, hoping they take the hint. Their congratulations and acceptance of this ruse while in a public setting needs to be believable.

Thankfully, they rise slowly from the table and shower us in their most genuine show of congratulations. Both offering a hand to Gabe, he takes them one by one and shares his gratitude with a bro hug. Jarett pulls me into a hug. "Congratulations, sis." He holds me tightly, whispering in my ear for only me to hear, "I don't like this, but for you, I'll accept whatever decision you make."

"And that's why you're my favorite brother," I whisper emotionally.

"I heard that." Roman laughs when Jarett lets me go. "You know she tells me the same thing, J." Rolling my eyes at them, I accept Roman's embrace. "Who would've thought you'd be the first," he gushes, squeezing me tightly. He looks me in the eyes, his hands cupping my shoulders when he pulls back from our hug. "Promise me you'll do what's right for you in the end."

Tears spring to my eyes unexpectedly. "I promise."

"Okay, let's toast to this union and officially welcome Gabe to the family." Roman's announcement is unexpected, but I follow his gaze around the speakeasy and see we have the attention of most of the customers. Some with their phones in hand, cameras no doubt at the ready.

"Thank you," I whisper, without moving my lips as I scoot into the booth between Roman and Gabe.

Right on time, Maxine joins us with a bottle of champagne and a glass for all.

Once we toast to our future together and Maxine and Kassidy have oohed and aahed over my cluster of diamonds, the crowd returns to their own business.

Now the real discussion begins.

"Did it occur to you to ask for my sister's hand in marriage?" Roman glances around me to Gabe, his expression serious.

Gabe returns his glare with valor. "No, it did not. With all due respect, she's not yours to give away." A silent tension builds between them, and I'm literally stuck in the middle.

Roman breaks first, and his laughter replaces all the hostility surrounding us. Gabe follows suit, and lastly, Jarett joins them. Kassidy, Maxine, and I share an amused glance. "I like him, Soph. He can hold his own." I sigh with relief and squeeze Gabe's leg beneath the table.

"Be good to her, and I'll stay out of your business.

We *both* will." He emphasizes the last few words, his eyes darting to Jarett, who nods in agreement.

"I have to ask…" Jarett adds, his voice low, "… the ring, the public proposal, the wedding date announcement, it's all part of the… show, right?"

Gabe covers my hand, interrupting me before I'm able to confirm or deny. "Where Sophia is concerned, yes. For me, it's less for show and more about my true feelings. I'm in love with your sister, have been for over a year, and I won't apologize for it."

"I knew it!" Kassidy bounces, clapping her hands together.

"Calm down, love," Jarett warns her sweetly.

"You made that comment to the press to strong-arm her into marrying you?" Jarett whispers harshly, leaning over the table, his hands clenched in fists and knuckles white with tension.

"Absolutely not, but you believe what you will."

Roman remains quiet for a beat, staring between Gabe and me, ignoring Jarett's reaction.

"Once you told the world you were marrying my sister, you what? Suddenly realized you wanted forever with her?"

Gabe chuckles softly. "I've been pushing for more for some time now, but your sister is loyal to the walls she's built around her heart. I intend to break them down with mad love and proper intentions." He lifts my hand to his mouth and brushes a tender kiss across my knuckles. Staring deep into my eyes, he adds, "You own my heart, and one day, I hope I'll own yours."

This makes Roman smile, Kassidy's jaw drop, and I swoon from my head to my feet, falling a little deeper in lust with Gabe Lugreno.

And I do something I've never done before.

Taking Gabe's face in my hands, I lower his lips to mine.

For the first time in my life, I let go of all expectations and inhibitions and follow my heart without a fuck in the world. And if it's not the best feeling in the world, I'm done with life.

Losing myself in our kiss for a few long seconds, Roman clears his throat subtly behind me.

Gabe's shit-eating grin brings me back to reality as we break apart. Yeah, he shattered another piece of my armor and weakened a thousand more.

Even the strongest walls are made to be broken.

"On that note, my break is over. I'll be right back with cocktails for everyone." Maxine dashes to the bar to put her exquisite craftsmanship to work, and this is about to become a real celebration.

"I believe Sophia has other news to share with you too." Gabe hints, reminding me to share our new living arrangements before I heed more concerned calls about why I won't open my door.

"Yes, Gabe… no, *we*, have moved."

"Moved where?" Jarett bites out.

"Not too far, we're still in the same area." It's one thing I'm grateful for. Gabe didn't insist we move out of the area away from my family. He knows how important they are to me.

"Let's just say we upgraded to a suite in the Sky Tower Resort in Shoreditch."

"The residential tower for the insanely rich?" Kassidy asks, her eyes wide and dreamy.

"Let me guess, you're not starting at the bottom and working your way up?" Jarett jokes, and Gabe has the audacity to look offended.

Laughing, I continue. "Yes, the Sky suite is their elite penthouse with rooftop garden access overlooking London. You all should come for dinner. Anyone know of a decent chef?"

Now it's Roman's turn to let out an offended gasp.

"Sounds like a plan," Maxine says, handing out the black beers for the guys and the decadent cocktails for Kassidy and me. "Cheers guys, I'm really happy for you both." A familiar look shared between her and Roman reminds me he has news of his own to share.

"Okay, enough about us. Roman, what's your news?"

His relaxed demeanor spikes a notch or two on the tension scale, and he glances again at Max. The table is silent, waiting for him to speak.

"Actually, I'm waiting on confirmation before I

divulge the top-secret news. I expected it today, but this time next week, I hope I'll have an exciting announcement of my own." His grin appears off, perhaps a little staged, and it's hard to miss the disappointment in Maxine's eyes as she excuses herself and returns to the bar.

"What was that all about?"

Roman shrugs. "Like I said, I need a few more days to secure the details."

Chapter 23

GABE
One Month Later

"Tell me you found something solid on this bastard, Ronnie."

"It's not been easy, but after a lot of digging into archives and breaching multiple privacy laws, I found his true identity."

It's been a month since I first contacted Ronnie to track down the guy asking questions about me in New York. Ben says he's not seen him since, and without a clear picture of the guy, he's proved difficult to trace. Due to the angle he was filmed at in the press release the day Sophia disclosed our wedding date and Ben's security footage falling short, he's been harder to find than a penny in the ocean.

"I'm not sure you're going to like what I've found,

Gabe. To be honest, if you've not heard from him directly in the past few weeks, it seems unwarranted to give you the news."

Ominous information isn't my style. "Ronnie, the details. Now."

The unsettling tone of his voice is enough to pour a glass of whiskey and settle in on the lounge in my office. "Don't say I didn't warn you."

"The name Dustin Hawthorne mean anything to you?"

Dark clouds are rolling in over the river, and I stare out over Central London, racking my brain trying to place the name but come up short. "No, should it?"

"What about Danny Thorne?"

Now that's a name I've seen recently. When I walked into Sophia's home office a few days ago, she was searching information on this man. I assumed it was client research.

My skin prickles at the possibility these men are one in the same.

"Not until now, but I believe Sophia has also been looking into him."

A sense of dread fills me as Ronnie says, "Is it possible he has reached out to her? It's the name he currently goes by."

Would Sophia have come to me directly if he had? I'm not so sure.

"And Dustin Hawthorne is his real name?" I question.

My computer pings with an email notification. "Open the link I sent you."

Returning to my desk, I open my email, and the blood drains from my face as the link connects to a news article from many years ago with a picture of a young boy crying, comforted by a much older woman. The headline reads, 'Three Dead in a Fiery Plane Crash.' It goes on further to say the five-year-old boy was left orphaned, to be raised by his father's estranged older sister whom he'd never met.

The boy's name is Dustin Hawthorne.

"Fucking hell."

Ronnie sighs heavily on the end of the line. "Yeah. Either he's after money or plans to ruin your life for the sins of your father. If I were you, I'd talk to Sophia immediately."

My eyes remain glued to the news report in front of me. As I scroll, my heart wretches. Images of Marcelle and Beverly Evans stare back at me, and hate for my father surges through my veins like rapid fire once more.

I'll never escape the evil he committed and the lives he ruined.

Instead, his decision may end up ruining the one thing I love more than success and money.

Sophia.

Ronnie promises to send all the info he has on Danny, including his most recent location. First, I hightail it over to Sophia's office, hoping she's not out with a client. I consider calling her first, but decide an impromptu visit is a better option.

In the time it will take me to walk to Incontro, I hope to have a plan in mind.

Sophia is sitting behind her desk when I walk through the doors. Her reading glasses poised on the end of her nose is a sign she's deep in concentration, reading or researching. Kelli is on the phone and waves me through.

"What do I owe the pleasure of a mid-morning visit?" Sophia asks, rising from her chair to greet me with a kiss. It's become our norm over the past few weeks. She's softening to the idea of sharing a home, and displays of affection are more comfortable than a sense of duty.

"Business, I'm afraid."

"Oh?" She frowns, signaling to take a seat opposite her.

"Who's Danny Thorne to you?"

A look of surprise washes over her at my abrupt question.

"Wha..."

"Don't play dumb with me, Sophia. You were googling the man only days ago."

Slamming her palms on the desk, she jumps from her chair and stares me down. "Be careful, Gabe. This is my place of business, and the one place I'll never answer to you."

Rounding her desk to close the door behind me, she yells to Kelli, "Please hold my calls."

With her back to me, she stops by the kitchenette to pour a cup of coffee without offering one to me. "Are you jealous of my client research, Gabe?"

"So, he's a client." Part of me breathes a little easier.

"Potentially, he could be."

"What does that mean?"

She turns to me, the scowl on her face would ordinarily have me backing away. It's never my intention to upset her.

"It means exactly what I said. Why the inquisition?"

Silence draws out between us as I consider my answer. "A client brought him to my attention today, and I recognized the name after seeing his name on your computer."

"Hmm, I see."

"Have you met with him yet?"

She shakes her head, "No, I haven't."

"Don't." I stand and button my jacket, preparing

to leave.

"Excuse me?"

I sigh. This woman is nothing if not strong-willed. "It's possible the man is trying to extort money from me. Until we know his end game, I forbid you to speak with him."

With wide eyes, Sophia walks to me. "Why would a reporter risk his job to extort you?"

"Reporter?" I frown.

Wrapped up in why she'd be researching this fucker on my walk over, I didn't check Ronnie's emails for further details. Perhaps I should have.

"Yes, he's American, too," she adds, a concerned look on her face tells me there's more.

"Sit down," she orders as she returns to her seat with her coffee.

She tells me about the day the reporters were swarming the entrance of the building. The day after our engagement went viral.

"And he spoke to you?"

"He stood at the back and asked something like, *do you know the real Gabe Lugreno?*"

Chills race the length of my spine. "And you didn't think that was odd?" I try to hide my annoyance, but her ignorance isn't always blissful.

"Of course, I did. Hence, why I reached out to some reporter friends to ask about him. I can't find much about him online, but he's been approaching local news channels under the disguise of being a freelance journalist from Connecticut."

In an attempt to avoid losing my shit, I hold in a deep breath, grinding my teeth together.

"Before you say anything more, I didn't know it was a *disguise* but now you're here, I'm guessing that's why I can't find any of his credentials."

"Until I get to the bottom of this and why he's asking around about me and my business, please don't engage with him." What I really mean is until I find this motherfucker and give him a large sum of cash to shut the fuck up, stay the hell away from him.

Better yet, forget he exists.

Chapter 24

SOPHIA
A Month Later

In complete darkness, I roll out of bed and race to the bathroom, only making it with seconds to spare. Groaning, I clutch my stomach as I heave into the toilet, my mind weary and my body shaking. *What the hell?*

When I finish, I clean myself up and take a hot shower to relax. It's not until I return to bed that I notice Gabe isn't in it. There's no sign of lights throughout the apartment, but I pull on my satin robe and go in search of him.

He's sitting in the dark on the balcony, staring out over the city, and doesn't hear me approach.

"Are you okay?"

Gabe doesn't answer. He barely acknowledges my presence with only a slight flinch at my broken whisper. My throat is scratchy from throwing up, and I feel lightheaded. Taking a seat in the lounge beside him, I try again, "I woke up sick, and you weren't there."

He glances at me. "I'm sorry, sweetheart. Can I get you something?"

Smiling, I shake my head. "No, I wondered where you were, is all. Is everything okay?"

"Of course. Let's get you back into bed."

I see the sweet side of Gabe more often now, though his controlling side will always be an issue for me, except in the bedroom. This man can dominate me any way he likes when we're both naked. My heart warms as he picks me up, cradling me to his chest, and returns to the bedroom.

"Are you coming back to bed?" I whisper as he tucks me in.

"I won't be long."

Quietly, he disappears, closing the door behind him. This business with Danny Thorne has been keeping him up at night, but last week he assured me he's no longer a threat. Unwilling to share any details with me, I took him at his word. But there's a feeling I can't seem to shake about this whole situation.

Why would a man show up at my work, pretending to be somebody he isn't, throw out a cryptic question, then avoid contact with Gabe for weeks, despite his best attempts. Then suddenly to hear all has been dealt with, and he's no longer a threat, things don't add up.

Perhaps my concern over the matter is what has my stomach in knots.

I sigh.

Or maybe it has more to do with my agenda for the day.

Glancing at my phone, I see it's two fifteen in the morning on the anniversary of my parents' devasting death. This day never gets easier for me, and it's probably the reason I've been so emotional this past week.

I'm falling in love with a man who has promised me the world. Twelve months from now, I'll be waist-deep in wedding preparations, and I'd give anything to have my parents with me. The times this past month I've wanted to talk to my mom about Gabe, my first real love, have been too numerous to count.

A love I never thought I'd experience. Despite my best efforts, my walls are crumbling, and I know without a doubt, I'm in love with this man. It both terrifies and excites me.

Though it's a conversation I'll never get the chance to have with my mom, it breaks my heart.

Tears well in my eyes and run down my cheek as I close them. Memories of the last time I saw my parents alive fill my mind. I kissed them both goodbye and promised them I'd look after my brothers in their absence.

Jarett was only sixteen, Roman twenty-four, but he was living on the wild side by then. College parties were more important than family obligations, and he spent his nights sleeping his way through the city to forget about the girl next door who he'd loved since he was a boy.

Maxine.

Every day, I have kept my promise and looked out for my brothers as they have always done for me. And today, my brothers and I will meet at three o'clock at the cemetery as we've done every year since our parents' death.

It was that time twenty years ago today, the local police stood at the door of our family home and delivered the news that turned our lives upside down. They left us billions of dollars, a gorgeous family home on acreage, and I'd give every bit of it back, and more, to still have them with us today.

When Gabe makes his way into bed, he wraps me in his arms, and I fall apart. Sobbing, I allow him to cradle me, knowing he understands more than most and won't push me to talk about it.

Eventually, I drift off to sleep, and when I wake, daylight filters through the window. As I begin to stir, the slight movement churns my stomach, and I make a mad dash to the bathroom once again.

"Maybe you should take today off," Gabe suggests as I prepare for work. As always, I intend to have breakfast at my mom's favorite diner from when we were kids, go to the office for a few hours, pick up my flower order and a new angel charm to hang on their headstone, and make my way to the cemetery.

"I told you, I have a regime to get me through this day. I'm not changing it because I ate something bad last night."

"Sweetheart, I ate the same meal as you did, and I'm fine. You're emotional."

"Yes, Gabe. I'm emotional. It happens, and I'll get over it," I snap as I step into my heels and thread my diamond hoops through my lobes. Not in the mood to be comforted, I shrug out of his attempt to embrace me from behind. If I allow him to hold me right now, I'll be as good as screwed for the day.

"I'm sorry, I didn't mean to snap. I need to get going."

"I love you, Sophia. Are you sure you don't want me to go with you today?"

It's on my lips to say the three words I know he's dying to hear from me, but today isn't the right time. He deserves to hear them when I'm at my happiest, bubbling over with joy. And joy isn't something I feel right now.

"No, but thank you. I'd love you to meet us for drinks at Maximum afterward, though?"

"I'll see you there." He brushes a kiss over my lips, and I step out of our apartment ready to take on the day.

The thought a high-protein breakfast and a strong coffee will settle my tummy makes me a fool. Halfway to the office, I double-over, head in a stinking trash can, and bring up my entire meal and then some. Wiping my hand across my face, I dig in my bag for sanitizer and a breath mint, appalled at myself. Passersby openly stare and curse my vile actions.

I struggle to keep myself upright. My body is shaking violently, either the result of the stomach bug or shame, I'm not sure.

Pushing my way through the doors of Incontro, Kelli instantly follows me to my office. Closing the door behind us, she shrieks, "What the hell happened to you?"

After telling her of my humiliation on my way in, she chastises me for coming in today. "I'm calling Gabe."

"No, please don't. Pretend I'm not here. Pull my blinds and hold my calls," I say as I ditch my heels and lay on the sofa.

Kelli huffs but knows better than to argue. "In the event I fall asleep, please wake me at one o'clock." She agrees and covers me in a throw before fetching some water to place on the side table.

"Thank you."

"Oh, and this came for you after you left

yesterday. Private courier," she says, picking up a large envelope from my desk. "There's no name, but it's addressed to you and marked confidential."

"Ugh," I groan, waving at her to leave it there. "I'll look at it later."

Chapter 25

GABE

"You smug son of a bitch. I gave you what you wanted."

Clutching the phone in my iron fist, I see red. If I ever get my hands on this cunt, I'll end him.

"No, asshole, you gave me pennies compared to what you're worth to keep me quiet."

Frustration seeps from my pores.

"Name your price," I grind out.

When a sadistic laugh filters through the line, I toss a dart at the board across from my desk.

"You don't get it, do you? I don't want your money. My old man left me with more than enough. But what five-year-old needs millions of dollars in his piggy bank? A father is worth more than any dollar amount you could ever offer. And yours took mine away."

We've done this dance a dozen times now. I throw money at him, and he comes back for more. Now he's saying he doesn't want it. Fuck me, I promised Sophia this bastard was gone from our lives, then suddenly he's calling me in the middle of the fucking night while I'm in bed with the woman I love.

The woman who'll never forgive me for lying to her.

For hiding who I am.

I won't let this fucking asshole ruin my life, despite what my father did to his.

"My father's sins aren't my own. Trust me, I lost my father that day too."

Another wicked laugh pushes me over the edge.

"Listen here, asshole, I don't know what your end game is, but stop hiding behind your fucking phone and tell me what you really want."

"I want you to suffer like I did. An orphan at five and taken advantage of by the woman who was supposed to care for me. Yeah, I'll never have a Sophia in my life, I'm too fucking scarred. But you... you're living your best life as if you're not bred from the scum of the earth. Tell me, *Gabriel Bartholomew* of Connecticut, how do you think Sophia will feel when she finds out what you've been hiding?"

Son of a bitch!

"You stay the fuck away from her."

"Too late. It's a glorious day for a family

gathering at the cemetery, don't you think?"

The phone goes dead, and I throw it across the room in my rage.

Not today. This can't fucking happen today. Of all days, this will break Sophia.

Picking up my phone, I race from my office and yell at Elise, "Have Viktor meet me out front." It's rare for her to work with me in London these days. I mostly have her running the headquarters in New York. Confused, she yells back as I enter the elevator. "Will you be back?"

"Not today," I answer as the doors close, and my heart nearly explodes from my chest.

I consider calling Sophia but don't want to interrupt her family moment. And for all I know, this asshole, Danny, or Dustin, might be calling my bluff.

Viktor is pulling to a stop as I exit the building, and I jump in the back seat. "The cemetery."

Fifteen minutes later, we turn off the main road and drive slowly through the gates of the cemetery. I have no idea where they are, but I'm on the lookout for a man who doesn't belong near my woman.

"Up ahead, Sir?" Viktor points to three people gathered around a grave, fresh flowers lighting up an otherwise dark day.

"Slow down," I say when a vehicle sneaks in from the other direction.

It appears to stop, and we wait to see if anyone exits the car. Viktor parks us between the trees, a way back from where Sophia is now crouched over her parents' grave. Shielded by the trees, I'm unsure if the occupants in the other vehicle can see us, but I'm sure we can't be seen from where the three most important people in my life are standing.

Half an hour later, Sophia, Jarett, and Roman leave, passing the car parked to the side of the road up ahead. As we pull out, a man exits the vehicle with a white envelope and places it on the headstone. Glancing in our direction, he gives a swift nod.

Motherfucker.

"Drive."

As we approach the area, the town car hums past us, windows down, and the sly son of a bitch grins at me. My fingers clench the door handle so hard it might break off in my hand.

"Glad you could make it. I'll see you at Maximum."

Words can't express the level of loathing in my blood for this man and his apparent hatred for me. The sick bastard wants to see me sweat, and fuck, if I'm not blinded with guilt already. Viktor pulls over and keeps the engine running while I collect the message he left for me.

On the front, the words *Copy Number Two* are

scrawled in black ink. I return to the car and direct Viktor to Maximum while I pull the contents from the envelope. Multiple copies of newspaper clippings about the crash are amongst a photocopy of my original birth certificate, change of name petition, and a photo of my father and me at his sentencing.

It's the last time I ever saw my father alive. The photo was taken as he hugged me goodbye before he was ordered from the courtroom and thrown inside a maximum-security prison upstate. I never visited him because I couldn't stand to look at the man.

When I heard of his death six months later, I wasn't surprised, nor did I cry for the death of the man I no longer knew. It wasn't hard to imagine he'd gotten mixed up with more than the deal which killed three innocent people.

Karma took him in the end—bludgeoned to death outside his cell by another inmate. That day, there was one less monster in the world.

But I now realize my father's actions created another monster twenty years later—one intent on ruining me for the actions of my father.

As we enter the street, I see Danny Thorne leap from the town car and enter the wooden doors. My legs bounce, willing the traffic to speed up. I have no idea what he plans to do or say when he gets inside, but I don't want Sophia hearing the worst without me present.

The moment we're close enough and the car slows to a near stop, I jump out and run the rest of the way.

"Gabe," Sophia rushes to me and throws her arms around me as I enter the speakeasy.

Confused by her public show of affection and by the lack of her desire to kill me, I glance around in search of Danny. That's when I see him, sitting at the bar, a beer in hand and a cocky grin on his face. Slowly, he shakes his head and turns away.

But not before Sophia follows my gaze and recognizes him. Her body tenses as she pulls away from me. "What's going on?"

"I'll explain later, I promise." I take her hand and lead her to the booth, signaling to Maxine for our usual drinks. I choose to sit on the opposite side of Sophia today to keep Danny in my sights.

Chapter 26

SOPHIA

After an emotionally draining day and a few drinks, I fall into bed earlier than usual. Gabe is quiet and appears to be carrying the weight of the world on his shoulders but refuses to talk about it. I decide to let it go, knowing he'll tell me more about the Danny situation tomorrow, we make love until I'm spent and struggling to keep my eyes open.

When Gabe's phone sounds in the middle of the night, waking me from my slumber, two things happen. First, my skin crawls, my senses on high alert that something is wrong, and two, my stomach threatens a repeat of yesterday morning as I roll onto my side.

An hour passes, and Gabe doesn't return to bed. My tummy has settled provided I don't move, though sleep evades me wondering if the phone call has anything to do with Danny Thorne. Knowing he was in the same establishment irked me, but Gabe convinced me he had everything under control.

For now.

But what the hell kind of business does Gabe have to deal with in the middle of the night? It's then I remember he has business dealings worldwide—the majority located in the United States—and time zones make his working hours difficult.

Maybe he's considering his move here to be more complicated than he anticipated. What if he decides my suggestion to stage a public breakup and call the wedding off is the best way for us to move forward after all?

Could I handle him leaving me? The thought causes tears to spring to my eyes.

Despite all the anti-engagement talk and fighting him at every turn about being in a *relationship, I love him.* He might not know it, but my heart belongs to him, and if he leaves me now, I'm scared I'll lose myself.

A short time later, sleep threatens to pull me under. Gabe tiptoes to our room, and I pretend to be asleep. I feel him above me, watching me in the darkness, and slowly he pulls the covers up to my chin and kisses my hair. "I love you, Sophia Evans," he whispers. "I only hope you can love me for *me.*"

Quietly, he leaves the room. He's not coming

back to bed. And he believes I don't love him.

My heart aches for him, and what may come if I don't tell him exactly how I feel.

But the heavy beating in my chest finally lulls me to sleep.

And I dream of him, of our wedding, and suddenly, the dreams end and another begins. When I wake, Gabe is gone.

He left me in the middle of the night.

Gasping for air, I lurch from the mattress, my hair matted together around my face. My vision is unfocused, and I scan the room for Gabe. "Sweetheart, are you okay?"

Sucking in a deep breath, my body begins to relax as he wraps his arms around me and lowers me back to his chest.

"You're still here," I cry.

Literally.

Tears spill from my eyes in an emotional frenzy onto his naked chest.

"Of course, I'm not going anywhere. Did you have a bad dream?"

A few moments of silence pass while I gather my thoughts. I prop myself up on my elbow, ready to ask him about the phone call and tell him about my dream.

And most importantly, confess how I truly feel about him.

But my stomach lurches in my throat as my head

spins, and I can't scramble from the bed fast enough.

Gah! What the fuck is wrong with me?

Gabe follows not far behind and lovingly holds my hair back while I'm head down in the toilet for a second day in a row. Since when do relationships have you vomiting on daily? This isn't my idea of a romantic emotional connection.

When I'm convinced I have nothing left in me, I push back on my heels, and Gabe pulls me upright. He prepares the shower while I brush my teeth. When we both step beneath the warm water, Gabe whispers with concern, "Two days in a row, Sophia. This is definitely not food-related."

"Yesterday was an emotional day, and given how I woke up today, I'd say emotions are to blame."

Leaning against Gabe's chest, I let the water pour over the front of my body. "You want to tell me what this morning's panic attack was all about?"

Panic attack.

I've never been prone to stress in my life. I take the shit life dishes out as a chance to grow, challenging myself with every shitty hand I've been dealt. To be better. More.

"It wasn't a panic attack," I say, turning to face him.

"Whatever it was, tell me what had you so worked up. You were sobbing in your sleep, then suddenly you sat up, gasping for air."

He begins to lather soap over my body, caressing me softly as I explain my dream to him. "I'm not going to leave you, sweetheart."

"You've not been yourself, and you didn't come back to bed after your phone call."

"Turn around."

Gabe finishes washing my back. "Do you want to discuss your phone call?"

"No, I'm more worried about you."

Shaking my head against him, I remain silent, confused as to why I feel so knackered every day.

"I want you to stay home today. You can arrange with Kelli for me to go into the office and collect anything you need, and you can work from bed."

"Gabe..."

"Please, don't fight me on this."

Instead of arguing or pleading my case, I turn to him and lock my arms around his neck. "Gabe," I start, pulling back to look in his eyes, "I love you."

A smile lights up his eyes in a way I wish I'd told him long ago. "I'm sorry I fought you so long. I was scared."

"And now?"

"Now, I'm scared to lose you."

Chapter 27

GABE

The words I've longed to hear finally leave her lips, and I'm so preoccupied with the threat of losing her, it's hard to feel good about it.

Danny fucking Thorne called me in the middle of the night. He hinted at leaving a package for Sophia but seeing us both together at Maximum, it was clear to him that she hadn't received it. I assume it's package number one with copies of the same contents I received.

Proof of what I've been hiding, the exact information that will tear Sophia and me apart. I need access to her office to run interference and make sure that package is never discovered. Thankfully, she agreed to stay home today and let me pick up some things for her. I only hope Kelli allows me into her office to look for myself.

Once I find it, I need a plan B to get rid of this asshole once and for all.

"Ronnie," I rush the moment he answers the call. "Tell me you've found something on this bastard I can use against him."

"I'm afraid not. He's a loner, Gabe. There's nobody important to him, he has struggled with a gambling addiction for years, and it looks like he used your payoff to settle the last of his debts. It seems he's a drifter with no ambition."

"No, his ambition is to ruin my life the way my father ruined his."

Viktor gazes at me through the rearview mirror as we approach Incontro. He knows a little of my story, but not all of it.

"I suggest you come clean with Sophia, son. It's the only way. Tell her before he does."

Because he'll tell her everything. Ronnie doesn't say it, but we both know this is how it will end.

My secret getting out won't only destroy my relationship, it could have a severe negative impact on my business. If investors get wind that I've hidden my true identity, regardless of its impact on my business, my name will be dragged through the mud, and I'll lose all credibility.

Unless I act first.

"Hello, Kelli." I grin, walking through the doors of Incontro.

"I'm worried about her, Gabe. Sophia doesn't get

sick, not even at this time of year."

I can't help but wonder if Sophia's concern is elevated by my lack of emotional presence lately. "You and me, both. That's why I'm here to collect some work for her. It's best she's out of the office for a few days until whatever is causing these attacks goes away."

"Attacks?"

I sigh. "She woke with a panic attack this morning."

Kelli's concerned expression mirrors my own. "Go on…" she waves to Sophia's office, "… give her my love and make sure she knows we have everything under control here."

Nodding, I assure her, "She trusts you, Kelli."

Sifting through the documents she asked me to find, in search of…

"Gotcha," I whisper to nobody.

A large white envelope addressed to Sophia in the same scrawled ink as the one I received yesterday. So far, it remains unopened, and I breathe a sigh of relief.

Packing up her laptop, calendar and the paperwork she requested, I load up her briefcase which she *never* leaves in the office and make my way out. Grateful for once she's let her guard down and left everything she needs at the office, gives me a solid reason to be here snooping around.

With the envelope tucked inside my jacket, I

thank Kelli for her assistance and step outside. While I wait for Viktor to return and collect me, I call Elise and apologize for running out on her yesterday.

"There's one more thing I need you to do."

When I request her to arrange an interview with the *New York Times*, she does something she's never done before. Elise questions my plan.

"Gabe. Mr. Lugreno, is this something to do with Danny Thorne?"

My breath hitches in my throat, my airways closing in. "What do you know about Danny Thorne?"

"He's waiting for you in your office. I was just about to call."

Fuck.

"Stay with him. Don't let him out of your sight. I'm on my way."

"He knows, doesn't he?"

"Yes."

Elise has known since the day she started work for me that my legal name isn't my birth name. Until I started to pursue Sophia, she never knew why. Now, she knows everything.

Storming into my downtown London office building, I have one thing on my mind. To finish this once and for all.

"Thank you, Elise," I growl as I step into my office, my eyes focused on Danny.

Once Elise leaves us alone, I stalk across the room, filled with rage, and pull Danny Thorne to his feet by his cheap Walmart collar. Driving him into the nearest wall, I seethe through gritted teeth. "The fuck kinda game are you playing at?"

Dropping him to his feet but not letting go, his slimy grin spreads across his fucked-up face. His eyes are void of emotion, his soul void of empathy.

"I told you we'd be meeting soon. You shouldn't underestimate me, *Gabriel.*"

My skin crawls at the mention of my real name. The name my mother gave me. Lugreno was her maiden name which I happily took when I was looking for an alias and a fresh start.

"You can't hurt me. I have a tell-all interview booked with the *New York Times*, and Sophia will forgive me because she loves me."

His wicked laugh grates my last nerve, and I sucker-punch him in the throat. Gasping, he falls to the floor, hands around his neck but his grin never falters.

"You think a public declaration will make me go away? Even if Sophia doesn't leave you, I'll remain a *thorn* in your side forever." A choked laugh squeezes from his throat as he picks himself up off the floor. "See what I did there? I'm thinking of legally changing my name to Thorne, so you'll always remember what I am to you."

"You're a sick son of a bitch. You didn't deserve

what my father did, but I washed my hands of that monster the day I found out the truth. He ruined my life too."

What Danny fails to acknowledge is the pain from his actions affects all five of us. Five children were orphaned that day because of one shady deal and a desperate decision made by my father.

"Imagine her face when you finally tell her the truth. And she learns you're only telling her because you felt threatened by a nobody like me."

My fists clench at my sides, my desire to draw blood from this fucker is almost too much to bear. "Ben didn't take it too well when my colleague filled him in today. Thinking all these years since college that he was your best mate, only to learn he didn't even know your real name."

Bullshit. This has nothing to do with Ben, and it changes nothing. But it's time to fly home and secure some loose ends.

First, I need to tell Sophia.

Chapter 28

SOPHIA

Gabe calls to say he'll be longer than expected as something urgent needs his attention at his office. Unsure whether it has anything to do with Kassidy's assignment, I attempt to call her. When she answers the call on the first ring, I burst into tears.

"Sophia? Honey, what's wrong?"

"I don't fucking know. I'm throwing up, waking with panic attacks, and I just told Gabe I loved him."

"O-kay," she answers slowly. "Are you at home?"

I tell her Gabe has sentenced me to work from home today, and I'm waiting on my things from the office.

"I'm on my way over."

When the queen of lattes shows up at my doorstep twenty minutes later, she has two oversized cups of coffee and offers me a sympathetic smile. The aroma of coffee assaults my senses, and my stomach churns again.

"Are you going to be sick again?"

I wave at the coffee, swallowing hard to keep from heaving.

Kassidy walks to the kitchen and places the cups on the counter and returns to me with a bottle of water from the refrigerator. "Here, you don't look so good."

Taking the water from her, I risk a few small sips.

"Come on, let's sit down." We settle on the sofa in the living room, and Kassidy turns all serious. "What's really going on, Sophia?"

I tell her about Danny Thorne, Gabe being distant, my dream, and this morning's panic attack.

"And you've been sick the past two mornings as well as unusually exhausted and overly emotional."

She stares at me curiously and I roll my eyes at her. "Yes, Kassidy, I'm a wreck. Thank you for pointing it out."

"You're not a wreck, Sophia. Is it possible you could be pregnant?"

My eyes widen, and a laugh escapes me. "Pregnant? Are you crazy?"

Her pointed stare remains unnerved by my reaction. "I can't be pregnant, Kass. I'm too fucking old to have kids."

"You're forty, Sophia, not eighty, and whether

you want to be or not doesn't really matter. Is it a possibility?"

"Of course not, I'm on the pill, and..."

"And what?"

Thinking back to my last period, my head begins to spin as I recollect the one pro I listed when considering a fake married life with Gabe.

Sex on tap.

We agreed when we started living together, or rather, when I was *moved* in with him, there was no need for condoms. But I've never missed a day of the pill, except the first morning I woke up in this suite with Gabe. The morning after our engagement video went viral, and I bounced out of bed to answer Jarett's call, demanding answers.

"I need a calendar."

Kassidy hands me her phone, and I open the app, counting backward to my last cycle. Even as I bypass the previous month, I know it's useless. I haven't had a cycle since I moved in here.

Tears cascade over my cheeks, my semi-damp hair in a messy bun on top of my head bouncing as my body shakes uncontrollably.

"How could I miss this?"

Kassidy pulls me to her and shushes me. "You've had a lot on your mind lately."

"This was never part of my plan, Kassidy. You don't understand."

"A fake engagement and falling in love with the

man you never intended to marry wasn't part of your plan either. Plans change, Sophia."

We sit in silence for what feels like hours before Kassidy finally suggests making a doctor's appointment. But I'm not sure I want confirmation until I can wrap my head around the possibility.

"Wouldn't you rather know? It could be the added stress messing with your cycle. Hell, you might be going through early menopause."

Now she has my attention. "I'm *not* menopausal," I screech at her.

Kassidy shrugs. "Until you see the doc, how do you know?"

Sighing, I know she's right. "I don't want Gabe to know. Not until I know for sure."

An hour later, I'm waiting for my GP with Kassidy by my side for strength. I might feel like I've been run over by a freight train, but if a pregnancy test shows up positive, I may well run out in front of one.

"Sophia Evans," the nurse calls my name, and hesitantly, I follow her to the doctor's office. When Kassidy isn't hot on my heels, I spin around and summon her inside with me. Without question, she sits by my side, her hand on my arm for support as I explain the past few weeks.

"So, you aren't actively trying to get pregnant?"

"Definitely not. I've never considered having children." Not since my parents died, at least.

Dr. Lafferty pricks my finger and dabs the blood with a testing strip. "I don't even get to pee in a cup?" I try to laugh, but humor is beyond me.

"We have much quicker and easier testing methods these days. Let's get you up on the bed, and I'll examine your tummy."

Glancing at the strip on her desk, I wonder how long until my fate will be decided. As if reading my mind, she says, "It will take a few minutes."

Cold fingers poke at my lower abdomen. "I'd like to do an internal examination. If you could remove everything from the waist down, please."

Panic looms, and I glance over at Kassidy. "Is there something wrong?"

The doctor spins a radiology machine around near my head and prepares a lengthy dildo-shaped probe with gel after checking the test strip and discarding it. "No, but you *are* pregnant."

Forgetting how to breathe, my head spins violently, and I'm on the verge of passing out.

"Deep breath, Sophia." A paper bag is supported at my mouth, and the doctor's words pull me from my state of sheer panic.

"This is the second panic attack today?" she asks, glancing across at Kassidy for confirmation.

"I believe so, yes."

"Relax, Sophia. I want you to focus on your breathing and keep using the bag while we have a look at what's going on."

Ten minutes later, Dr. Lafferty orders me to get dressed and asks Kassidy to slip out and get me a cup of water. "I'd say you're about six weeks along, and given your elevated levels of exhaustion and the panic attacks, I'm going to write you a prescription for some pre-natal vitamins and suggest you visit a psychologist."

"I *am* a psychologist," I groan, hating I'm in this position.

"Then you know how important it is to talk to someone outside of your personal situation. I'm a doctor, Sophia, it doesn't mean I can diagnose and treat myself. We, as professionals, need the advice and guidance of others in our field from time to time. And your time has come."

Kassidy enters the room with water, and I chuckle absentmindedly. "Six weeks pregnant and in need of a psych. Who would've thought?" I joke.

Sympathy pours over me from both directions as I try to push back the tears invading my vision. "This can't be happening."

"I suggest you consider your options, have a read through this material, and see someone as soon as possible."

Taking the pamphlets, I thank her for ruining my life. Well, I didn't outright say it, but when the words left my mouth, that's exactly what I was thinking.

Chapter 29

SOPHIA

Gabe is waiting for me when I return home from the clinic.

"Where the fuck have you been? We need to talk," he snaps as I walk through the door.

"I went to see the doctor." I have no intention of telling him about the pregnancy yet, but I can't straight up lie to him.

"And?"

"She's prescribed some pills for my *panic attacks*..." I say, using my fingers to emphasize the diagnosis, "... and recommends I go talk to someone."

"Okay. Good." I frown when that's all he says.

"What do we need to talk about?" I ask, going through my briefcase to check he retrieved everything I asked for.

He hesitates, suddenly uncomfortable. "Never mind, you need to rest today."

"Don't treat me like some fragile doll about to break, Gabe."

"I'm not. I have some things to take care of in New York, and it's urgent. Come with me."

"Are you out of your mind? I feel like fucking shit, Gabe. Travel isn't what I need right now."

A frustrated sigh, and he's grappling his five o'clock shadow as if he wants to remove it with his bare hands. "I don't want to leave you alone."

"Gabe, I'm fine. I've organized with Kelli to work from home for the rest of this week."

I consider telling him Kassidy came with me today, and I could call on her if I needed anything, but the truth is, I've always been an independent woman, and today's results don't change that.

The next day, I manage to keep down my lunch after my breakfast smoothie forces me back to bed with a bucket by my side. According to my instructions, I have a phone appointment with a psychologist this afternoon, a colleague I trust immensely and have worked with in the past. But not on a personal level.

Not having heard from Gabe since he messaged to say he arrived yesterday, I'm not sure what to make of it. Tonight is our family night at Maximum, and I'm unsure how to attend without disclosing my news. After all, a pregnant woman shouldn't be drinking cocktails like water, and showing up with a sparkling water is only asking for questions I'm unwilling to answer.

Roman finally wants to tell us about his big news after putting it off multiple times over the past few months. I know I must be there for it, but I wish Gabe were here too.

If someone told me three months ago that I'd be pregnant, engaged, and wanting a man by my side for any reason, I'd have laughed in their face at their foolishness.

Now I'm the fool.

Knocked-up at forty.

When I hang up from my over-the-phone assessment, I have a missed call and a message from an unknown caller. First, I add tomorrow's in-person appointment to my calendar and try not to overthink what the session may reveal.

Opening the message, I tap on the image appearing to be a screenshot of a news report in the *New York Times. Billionaire Investment Mogul Tells All in an Exclusive Interview with NYT.*

What the hell?

Rushing from my office with my laptop, I turn on

the television, sifting through the channels to find the global news in case they're running the exclusive now. Tapping the headline into Google on my laptop, I wait for the results to load and click on the first article I find.

A tell-all interview has been filmed today with Gabe Lugreno, but the broadcast won't be aired until Sunday evening in the United States. Reports hint at whether the exclusive interview is aimed at his personal or business life.

Questions are raised in the comments about our engagement. Is it all for show or will Gabe's business ventures be outed for shady deals?

Will this be the demise of Lugreno Enterprises?
A Sneak Peek at the Billionaire's True Identity will be Revealed.
Is the Tycoon's Engagement a Media Strategy?

Immediately, I pick up my phone and dial Gabe's number. The headlines, snide comments, and aloof speculations are made worse when the call goes directly to his voice mail.

Wondering if this has to do with his dealings with Danny Thorne, I revisit my research on him. But only after I try to call the number the message was sent from, I receive the message, *this number is no longer in use,* and my blood boils.

Something is wrong, but it's time to get ready to see my brothers.

I arrive at Maximum early to talk with Maxine privately before the others show. The bar is quiet, and Max offers to talk in her office. "I don't know how to tell you this and also request that you don't ask any further questions."

"Oo-kay," she frowns.

"All my drinks from now until I say otherwise... I pause, unable to believe these words are about to come out of my mouth, "... please leave out the alcohol."

"Umm, wha... are you pregnant?" she whisper-yells, her eyes wide with shock.

Believe me, not half as shocked as I am.

"I can't deal with questions from Roman and Jarett right now, and Gabe doesn't know. Please, can you prepare my drinks as usual but without the liquor, so I don't have to answer questions or lie to the people I love?"

"Of course, anything for you. And I'm here if you need to talk about it."

Shaking my head, I thank her. "I can't talk about it yet, not until I come to terms with how I feel about it."

"I understand." She smiles. "There's been something I've wanted to share for some time, but when I talk myself into it being the *right time*, the universe seems to have other plans and things to get in the way. But when you know, you know, and we have to trust that time will come."

As I hold her gaze, I narrow my eyes. "That's cryptic."

She shrugs, a sorrowful smile on her lips. "I guess we each have a secret for our own reasons."

We hug, knowing nothing mentioned between us will ever leave her office. Maxine has been a part of our life, our family for as long as I can remember. Roman used to force me to visit and play with the older girl next door, just so he'd have the chance to come across and fetch me. It took years until I learned that was his game plan. Maxine knew all along.

Despite everything that's happened between her and Roman over the years, we have always remained close friends. *Sisters for life.*

Maxine returns to the bar to get started on our drink orders at the precise time the guys are due to show up, and I escape to the bathroom on my way. It turns out my excessive need to pee is also caused by my growing dilemma in my womb.

As I enter the speakeasy, the bar in my line of sight, I see Danny Thorne sitting at the bar with Jarett and Roman. All three of them are laughing at Max as she recounts a story, one I've heard a hundred times before.

"So-phi-a," Danny pronounces in three drawn-out syllables as I approach.

"I've been waiting for you." His wicked sneer sets off fireworks in my chest, and I glance at my brothers, who are yet to greet me.

"You two know each other?" Roman questions.

"No, but he's trying to extort money from Gabe."

The imposter laughs ferociously. "That's what he's told you about me? I don't want his money, Sophia."

With my arms crossed over my chest, I stare him down. "Then what exactly do you want?"

"Now all the family is here, I'd like to introduce myself."

Chapter 30

SOPHIA

Dustin Hawthorne.

"Wait," I shake my head, unable to make sense of his words. Why does that name sound familiar?

"Your name isn't Danny Thorne?"

His grin widens. "Not legally, but what's a name really?"

Roman stands and protectively situates himself between Dustin, Danny, or whatever the fuck his name is.

"Cut the bullshit. Why the introduction?"

"We have a lot in common, us four." I glance around to Roman and Jarett, who appear to be as confused as I am.

"Of course, why would my name have stuck in your memory? I'm a nobody from Texas, whereas you three became heir to the throne of the great

Marcelle and Beverly Evans."

Jarett pushes from his seat and pulls the man from his in one swift movement. "J," Maxine warns from behind the bar. He releases him immediately, and the slimy prick takes his drink and moves to our booth. He knows it's ours, he was here only days ago while we all sat at that very table.

Hesitantly, we follow his lead, and Maxine promises to bring my drink over in a moment and signals to the bouncer at the bottom of the stairs to keep an eye on us.

"Let's get one thing straight," Jarett starts as the three of us sit opposite him at the booth. "We don't care who you are, you'll never speak of our parents again."

Solemnly, he bows his head. "The name Simon Hawthorne mean nothing at all to you?"

I see the moment Roman connects the dots. "Simon Hawthorne was your father?"

"Yes, he was."

"Am I missing something here?" Jarett interrupts, and I, too, make the connection.

"His father was the pilot."

"Ah, now we're getting somewhere."

Jarett's bewildered expression matches my own, but he's first to lash out. "Is this some kind of joke to you?"

"Do I look like I'm joking? My father agreed to take that flight last minute because the usual pilot pulled out, and he needed the cash to feed his five-year-old son. But he never returned."

Tears fall from my eyes. "I'm so sorry, Dustin," I whisper the words sincerely, knowing the heartache that little boy has had to endure.

"Sorry?" he scoffs. "My father died because somebody wanted your parents dead. A broke man suffering at the hands of a wealthy firm fighting over their billions."

"You can't honestly blame any of us for your father's death. Our parents died in that same crash, you fucking asshole." Roman leans forward, his brow creased together and his jaw clenched tightly.

"Of course not." His smile is sinister and harrowing.

"What do you want from us?"

"I want nothing from you except to see your faces when you learn the truth."

Dustin shimmies across the seat and out of the booth, finishing the rest of his beer as Maxine delivers my mocktail. Fuck, I wish I wasn't on an alcohol-free diet.

"What truth?" Jarett pushes for an answer I know we're not going to leave here without tonight.

"All will be revealed by the end of the weekend."

We watch as he leaves the speakeasy, a place that has always felt like a second home. Right now, I feel violated and threatened in a place I've always felt safe and secure.

"What did I miss?" Kassidy asks, kissing Jarett and taking a seat opposite us. Jarett moves from my side to join her and fills in the blanks.

My mind wanders to the *New York Times* exclusive and wonder if it were him who'd sent the message earlier today. I check my phone and see Gabe has still not responded to my missed calls. I push my drink to the side. "I have to go."

"Where are you going?"

"Home." I don't want to worry them, but it's time I sorted through a box I've been unwilling to open since I packed it up almost two decades ago.

"Shit." I sit back down. "Roman, you were finally going to fill us in on your good news tonight."

He groans, and I'm quick to shut down the excuses. "Don't you dare say it can wait. We've been waiting months already. What is it?"

Maxine returns to the table and takes a seat. "Yes, Roman. It's time."

When you know, you know, and we have to trust that time will come.

Her earlier words ring in my ears. Roman's news has to do with Max. Is this what she's been struggling to share?

"Okay, fine. Maxine and I, we're..."

A smile lights up my face before he finishes the sentence. "Finally," I clap.

All eyes fall on me, and I excuse myself for my

outburst as Roman says, "We're going into business together."

Maxine glances at Roman, hurt visible in her eyes. That's not what she was expecting him to say.

"What about the café?" Jarett asks, and Maxine looks ready to leave the discussion.

"I'm bringing on a new chef for the café, and I'll continue to manage it as I've been doing. Max has a head chef position available here, and I've taken her up on the offer to branch out and put my skills to better use."

"That's excellent news, congratulations to you both."

They both accept my best wishes with a less than enthusiastic, "Thank you."

"When's all this happening?" Jarett asks, possibly pissed he's the last to know, considering he's Maxine's silent partner.

"A month from now," Maxine answers. "Now, if that's all the news, I'd better head back to work."

Roman nods. "It is, and thank you, Max."

Chapter 31

GABE

"Why didn't you tell me, man?"

Meeting with Ben was at the top of my list of things to do before I return to London. I'd intended to tell Sophia the truth before I left, but I was able to give the interview to the *New York Times* with the promise they wouldn't run it until Sunday. As soon as I leave Ben, I'm back on the jet bound for home.

And no more excuses. There will never be a *good time* to tell Sophia, but it must be done today.

"It's not as if I lied. Gabe Lugreno is my legal name. I changed it for a reason, to be rid of my father's name. What use would it be if I went around telling everyone my birth name?"

When I decided long ago to change my name, it was a personal decision to break away from my father's name. I didn't do it out of guilt for what he'd done but because I hated hearing his name, one that will, in my mind, always be associated with a monster.

"Look, I get it. But it was hard learning this from a stranger. I felt stupid not knowing, as if you couldn't trust me with the information."

"You shouldn't, and it's not about trust. I didn't do this to fool anyone into thinking I'm somebody I'm not."

"Yeah, yeah, I know."

We enjoy another round of beers before Henry reminds me it's time to get moving. "Always good seeing you, Ben. And thank you. For everything."

He offers me a hand, and I take it, bringing him in for a hug.

"Good luck with Sophia."

I'll take every bit of luck I find between now and then because fuck knows, I'm going to need it. "Thanks, man."

Sophia has been trying to call all day, and now I have the chance to respond, I can't get her to answer. I make a quick call to Kassidy.

"Gabe," she answers after a few rings.

"Hi, Kassidy, sorry to call you like this. I can't get hold of Sophia. Have you seen her?"

"She left Maximum an hour ago…" her voice fades, "… my guess is she's sleeping."

It's hard to miss the hesitation in her voice.

"What aren't you telling me, Kassidy?"

"Ugh, she'll kill me for saying anything to worry you, but a guy showed up tonight, said he was the son of the pilot who died alongside her parents. He was leaving as I arrived, but it shook them all."

My blood pressure skyrockets, but I hold my tongue.

"What else did he say?"

"I wasn't there, Gabe, but he mentioned the truth being revealed this weekend. Honestly, I don't even know if he's who he says he is. Reminds me of a money-hungry loser with a cross to bear."

"Thank you, Kassidy. I'll be home in a few short hours."

Ending the call, I walk into the cockpit. "We have an emergency. Let's get these wheels up now so I can get the hell home to my fiancé."

There's not enough Macallan 18 on this aircraft to settle my nerves. Sophia is still not answering as the doors close, and we prepare for takeoff. I phone Viktor and ask him to check in on her. "She requested I drop her to the old apartment, sir, after having me stop via the bank to retrieve some hefty filing boxes from her safety deposit boxes.

"She knows." The words are coarse as all blood runs from my face.

"I'm not sure what she does or doesn't know, but Danny Thorne walked out of Maximum tonight not long before she did. I'm sitting out front of her building to ensure he doesn't show up."

"Thank you, Viktor. I'll see you soon. Don't come for me, I'll Uber to you."

"Yes, sir."

I tap the window of Viktor's town car to alert him to my arrival.

"Have you seen her since she went up there?"

"No, neither of them."

Thankfully, I still have a swipe card for the apartment. We've been slowly redecorating it to use the place as a safe home for victims of domestic or sexual abuse. Sophia is colluding with her contacts through the Child Slavery Foundation she runs to open it for victims in need of a place to hide from their perpetrators while they seek legal counsel or other assistance they require.

Opening the door to her apartment, the only light is in the living room, where I find Sophia surrounded in paperwork. Files lay open on the floor around her, where she sits cross-legged on a cushion in the center of the room.

She doesn't hear me walk in, and I don't want to startle her. From where I stand, she appears defeated, overcome with sadness. Her tear-stained cheeks glimmer under the fluorescent lighting, and her eyes are blotchy and red.

"Sweetheart," I whisper. Her head spins in my direction, her eyes dark and outraged as they zero in on me.

"Don't you *sweetheart* me, you lying son of a bitch."

She makes no attempt to move as I walk into the room. The pain and suffering I've caused her are written all over her face. Newspaper clippings, photos of her parents, her family—all the childhood memories she has kept boxed away now cover the rug.

"Sophia, I can explain."

"You think an explanation for hiding your identity will suffice?"

"I never *hid* my identity, I just didn't *reveal* my past."

"Because you can't handle the truth or because you never wanted me to find out your father killed my parents?"

Running my hand through my hair, I close my eyes. "Both."

"Oh my God, Gabe. How could you lie to me about something this important?"

"Sophia, please…"

"No, Gabe. You don't get to ask anything of me ever again."

I shake my head. "I never lied to you. And I was going to tell you everything a few days ago, but you weren't well."

"How fucking convenient!" she snaps, crawling from her post on the floor and getting to her feet, an old newspaper article clutched to her chest.

"Is this you, Gabriel Bartholomew?" She shoves the article in my face, a mix of anger and sympathy in her bloodshot eyes.

Chapter 32

GABE

It's a photo of me at fifteen, shortly after charges were filed against my father for his involvement in the crash. At the time, I thought it was the second worst day of my life when three officers visited our home and took my father away in cuffs. Second only to the day my mother died.

"Yes, that's me." I lift my eyes from the article and stare at the woman I'm in love with. The woman I've hid myself from and may now pay the ultimate price.

"I was fifteen. This photo was taken outside our home after returning from court the day my father's charges were read aloud, and bail was posted. This was the day I declared my father dead to me. I escaped that night and booked myself into the boys' home, begging for a safe place away from my father."

"You felt unsafe with him?"

I scoff. "No, never. But once I learned what he'd done, everything I thought I knew changed. And I wanted nothing to do with him. I used his charges and a wad of cash my father kept beneath his mattress to convince the lady at the group home to take me in."

"Is that why you changed your name, to remove yourself from his image?"

"From his image, his name, and what would come of his reputation. Once I turned sixteen the month after he went to prison, I changed my name. Shortened my first name to Gabe and took my mother's maiden name."

"Why did you hide this from me, Gabe?"

"It's not the best first date conversation, Sophia, and I liked you."

"You didn't know me! Did you think dating me out of pity or guilt would save your soul and redeem you of your father's sins?"

"His sins aren't my own!" I lash out, scrunching the paper in my hands and throwing the ball into the pile of mess on the floor.

"No, they're not. So why hide the fact you knew who I was."

"I thought I was protecting you, Sophia."

"No, Gabe. You were protecting yourself. You wormed your way into my life, pressured me into a relationship that was more than I wanted, lied to the press, moved my whole life into a home *you* chose to call *ours*, waited until I fell in love with you, and *bam!*" Her arms flail around as she yells at me, her words cutting us both.

She turns and crouches over the back of the sofa, her head in her hands. Her body shakes as painful sobs break through the silence. Tears blur my vision as I listen to her and remember all the nights I cried myself to sleep as a teenage boy, desperate to wake and find out it was all a dream. That my father was still the loving, caring, successful, and genuine man I'd always believed him to be.

That day never came, and this day wasn't supposed to either.

"Sophia," I whisper as I try to comfort her, rubbing my hand over the middle of her back.

"Don't touch me. I don't even know who you are," she spits, pulling from beneath my touch.

"Yes, you do. You know me better than I know myself. And fuck, I never wanted you to relive this pain and was trying to save you the heartache from revisiting all these memories." My eyes plead with her, begging for forgiveness.

"This *pain* is part of my life, and I live with it every fucking day."

"That's not what I meant, and you know it."

"I don't know shit anymore. How can I ever believe a word you say to me after this?"

"I never lied to you, Sophia."

"Omitting important life-altering facts is as good as lying, where I come from."

Knowing she's right, I nod.

"Let's go home and talk about it."

When she lifts her eyes to mine, I know she has no intention of coming with me. "No, Gabe. I'm not ready to go to our fake home and continue living our fake lives."

"There's nothing fake about my love for you."

Tears raging down her face, she wipes them away with the back of her hand. "I fell in love with you, now I don't..."

"Don't say it."

"I'm sorry, Gabe. I don't know how to be with you right now. I need some space."

I glance around the apartment, only half decorated and void of any personal belongings. "Sweetheart, you can't stay here."

"I know. But my brothers need to know what I've uncovered this afternoon before your *New York Times* story goes live."

Frowning, I consider asking how the hell she knew about the interview, but I have no right to ask questions. "Yeah, received the alert from an unknown number, and hours later, Danny or Dustin, shows up and tells us he can't wait to see the look on our faces when we learn the truth over the weekend. So, I assume he was the one who sent it."

"That creepy son of a bitch has your number?" So he didn't outright tell her but gave her all the clues to figure it out herself. Weak bastard.

"What does it matter? He's no threat to any of us, he just wants to see us all hurt the way he is. I think he blames us for his father's death, and I dare say, he'll never forgive you for your father's part in it."

"What about you?"

"I need space and time with my family to figure this out in my head."

Her strong will is one of the things I love about her, and it won't do any good to order her home with me.

"Promise me, you'll let Viktor drive you to your brothers. You might trust Danny, but I don't, and I need to know you're safe."

"I didn't say I trust him."

"You should know, my private investigator confirmed he was the one to leak our relationship to the press. And he made that dickhead reporter say I was a client by waving a huge wad of cash in his face. Once I show him the proof we have of the bribe, I'll slap him with a restraining order and a ticket home. He won't be any more trouble for any of us."

Silently, she nods. And I leave, knowing I can't expect anything more from her tonight.

But leaving without her is my worst nightmare.

Making a call to Jarett, I warn him she's coming with news that casts a dark shadow over my name. But I remind him to consider who I am as both a person and a business associate. "I love your sister with all that I am, and I'll fight for her forgiveness." I end the call before he can ask any more questions, hating that I won't be in the room to defend myself when she shares the news.

The secret I've done everything to keep from being spilled.

All I can do is trust our love is enough, and her brothers will come to understand my reason for keeping quiet. My past might have brought me to them, first Jarett when I approached him about a deal a few years ago and then Sophia. But the life Sophia and I have is as genuine as I'm the son of a killer.

Chapter 33

SOPHIA

In the guest bed at Jarett's, I wake in a lather of sweat and run to the bathroom, my hand covering my mouth. After a late night with Roman and Jarett discussing Gabe, his father, and reminiscing about our parents, my sleep was broken and my dreams brutal.

"Sophia, are you okay?" Jarett yells from the other side of the bathroom door.

"Yes, I'll be right out."

Washing my face and brushing my teeth, I'm sickened by the state of myself when I look in the mirror. Is it possible to age ten years in the space of a few days? I swear my puffy, red-rimmed eyes magnify the fine lines and wrinkles that were barely noticeable before.

"Are you sick?"

With all the secrets, I don't have it in me to keep another. Not from Jarett. Hell, who knows how long I'll stay here for, and he deserves to know the truth. The morning sickness will be difficult to hide, anyway.

"Yes, J, I'm pregnant." My casual delivery throws Jarett off, and it takes a second for him to catch up.

"Holy fuck, since when? Does Gabe know?"

"I found out a few days ago, and no, Gabe doesn't know yet."

We make our way to the kitchen, where I make a black tea, as coffee is no longer my friend.

"You're going to tell him, though, right?" I consider this a moment too long.

"Sophia, he's the father. You can't keep this from him."

"Calm down. Of course, I'm going to tell him. I just don't know when."

Jarett hugs me, bringing on the waterworks once again. I sniffle into his shoulder. "Are the tears something I should come to expect while you're staying here?"

"Yes, and regular visits to the bathroom." We both laugh, and it feels good.

"You're welcome to stay as long as you like, but you need to sort things out with Gabe."

"I need some time, J. How can I ever trust him?"

Roman and Jarett are both irritated that Gabe kept his connection to us hidden but understand his point of view despite it being a *dick move.* Their words, not mine.

The emotions it evoked were mixed and painful—it's not something I thought I'd ever have to relive. And this is exactly what Gabe was trying to avoid by keeping it a secret.

"With time, you'll learn that you can. But don't wait too long to make things right with him."

When we originally heard of the accident and their deaths, it was the most difficult time in my life. Learning of the foul play and investigation into the crash elevated the difficulty tenfold. It bought with it angry, hatred, unforgiveness, and questions nobody could answer.

The day Derek Bartholomew was sentenced for tampering with the engine with the sole intention of killing my parents, it was chillingly soothing. Finally, somebody was paying for the devastation and loss we endured.

The company's CEO who ordered Gabe's father to carry out the work was also charged and sentenced to prison, losing his company in the process. Although justice was served, it didn't change the fact my parents were never coming back.

"Why are you suddenly team Gabe?"

"I'm not. I'm team Sophia." He kisses my

forehead. "You love him, and he's crazy in love with you, sis. Don't let a bad judgment call tear you apart."

I nod silently. "When I can think of him without seeing the crash or thinking of Mom and Dad, I'll talk to him."

"Maybe it would be good to start there in your therapy session today."

"Yeah." He's right, of course.

Either I allow this to come between us, and I raise our baby alone, or I find a way to deal with it, so I can marry the man I've fallen in love with and raise our child together. There's only one option I'm willing to consider, but I need to deal with this at my own pace.

When I walk out of my appointment with the psychologist, I'm a weeping mess, but I feel about ten pounds lighter, and there's a small spring in my step. I'm so grateful for the professional relationship I have with Dr. Milan which enabled me to meet with her on a Sunday. Watching Gabe's interview tonight will be difficult, and I'm prepared for the onslaught of emotions that will come with it. Knowing I have another session tomorrow also helps.

Instead of going back to Jarett's, I stop by the suite to pack an overnight bag. Thankful to Kassidy for loaning me a sleep shirt and a change of clothes for today, I need a few things to get me through the next few days. I'm grateful to find Gabe not at home, and throw a few things into a bag, including my vitamins and the pregnancy pamphlets I'd kept hidden in my office.

With my briefcase and overnight bag in hand, I wait for my Uber to arrive downstairs. Halfway to Jarett's, I redirect the driver. When I left my apartment after sending Gabe away last night, the floor was still covered in files. It's time to box them up for the final time.

The remainder of the day, I spend in my apartment and it proves to be therapeutic. Gabe's suggestion to turn the place into a safe home is a welcome reminder of the real man he is.

He gets me.

By the time I return to Jarett's, I'm starved.

"Roman, hey." I kiss my bro when I walk in, finding him hunched over the kitchen counter reviewing some paperwork.

"Hi, Soph, thought we could make a night of it, order takeout and watch Gabe's interview together." He shrugs, offering a sympathetic glance in my direction.

"Damn, I should've stopped for caramel popcorn on my way back," I add sarcastically.

"You seem brighter today. Did you speak with Gabe?"

"Not yet," I answer as Jarett and Kassidy walk through the door, the steamy aroma of Indian spices filling the room. As we prepare dinner, I give a run through of my day and discuss my therapy session along with the advice given to me.

"So, when you picture Mom and Dad, her recommendation is to picture Gabe as his fifteen-year-old self?"

"It seems odd, I know, but I think it helps."

"I saw him today," Jarett says. "He called to see how you were doing. The plonker was beating himself up but trying to give you the space you asked for."

Nodding, I'm grateful to hear he's thinking of me and giving me this time.

Jarett answers the knock at the door, and Maxine enters with a cheesecake in her hands. "Dessert has arrived," she announces cheerily, but her flamboyant smile dwindles when she sees Roman.

"Who's the sparkling grape juice for?" Roman asks as Kassidy sets the wine, juice, and five glasses on the table.

"Umm, I assume it's for me." I grin awkwardly, clutching my stomach. Roman's eyes drop to my hands.

"Are you kidding me... you're pregnant?"

"Yes. Are you ready to become Uncle Roman?"

Happiness washes over me as he hugs me. "Absolutely. Congratulations, sis."

Jarett turns the television on, and we begin to serve our meals as I answer all the questions about the pregnancy, Gabe, and the wedding. And I don't shed a single tear.

Chapter 34

SOPHIA

"The interview is about to start. Let's move to the sofa."

Lamb korma, beef vindaloo, and saffron rice—food has never tasted so good. Before I move, I unapologetically add another serving to my plate. Sitting on the three-seater between Max and Kassidy, I let out a deep sigh.

"We got you, lady." Maxine rests her dinner on her lap and squeezes my leg.

"Did Gabe give any idea what to expect when you spoke with him today, J?"

He shakes his head. "No. Only that he wanted to eliminate any doubt or risk of rumors about you, his relationship with you, and his business."

I hadn't considered the repercussions to his business, though his past in no way reflects who he is as a person or a businessman. My thoughts wander to Gabe and what he's doing right now. Is he watching too?

I miss him so much, my heart aches.

When Gabe's image fills the screen and the presenter introduces the segment, I wish he were here. We should be watching this together, standing as a united front. Seeing him sends a flutter through my chest.

We watch in silence as Gabe opens up about his past. He recounts the pain of losing his mother at a young age and the involvement his father had in the murder of our parents. The only sign of emotion is when he discusses his mother.

Gabe shares the reason for changing his name and the life lessons he navigated that made him the successful businessman he is today. He reiterates that every piece of information is available to the public, no records have been sealed, and vows he has nothing to hide. It was a decision made at the tender age of sixteen and one he has no regrets over.

When the presenter asks about our relationship, Gabe shifts in his chair. His expression softens, and a warmth invades his gaze. "The first time I met Sophia Evans, I knew exactly who she was. I never intended to start dating her, and falling in love wasn't even something I'd considered." He smiles into the camera as if he's looking directly at me, and my heart stops.

"In my early teens when I learned of the lives my father destroyed, I told myself I'd meet the Evans siblings and somehow repay them for their loss." He laughs, glancing at his feet. "It wasn't until I was older that I accepted nothing could make up for what they'd lost. It didn't stop me from wanting to meet them, though. I guess the orphaned part of me felt connected to them in some way."

Gabe's genuine responses to each of the questions asked speak to me deeply. His story moves me, a testament to the incredible man he is. "I fell in love with Sophia very quickly and completely unexpectedly. Because of her, my life will never be the same."

"How does she feel knowing your father caused her parents' plane to crash?"

"That's something only Sophia can answer, I'm afraid. I'd hate to speculate."

"So, you confirm Sophia knows and you're still together?"

The question visibly causes Gabe discomfort, but he answers without pause. "Sophia and her brothers are aware, yes. Sophia and I still plan to marry next September if I can't convince her to marry me sooner." I chuckle, a tear escaping the corner of my eye.

"Were you concerned she might leave you?"

"It's a lot for anyone to digest, but no, I have faith

in our love and the strength of our relationship."

"So, the engagement was real, and it wasn't a ruse to divert the media from accusations of Sophia sleeping with her clients?"

"To be clear, I'm the only client she was accused of sleeping with, and I've never been a client of hers or any other agency for that matter. We had been dating for a year at the time, and we weren't yet ready to announce our engagement to the world. A written apology was later published for the false information and unsubstantiated accusations. Our relationship is, and always has been, the real thing."

Shortly after, the presenter wraps up the story with a slideshow of images sharing our relationship.

"Sophia?"

"Hmm?" I turn to Kassidy. "Sorry, I was a million miles away."

"You doing okay?"

"Surprisingly, yes." I smile. It wasn't nearly as emotional as I expected it to be.

Forgetting my appetite as soon as my mind wandered to Gabe, I take my plate to the kitchen and cover my leftovers for later. At nights I'm particularly hungry after not being able to keep anything down throughout the day. Midnight snacks are my new best friend, and I secretly hope Maxine doesn't take all of the cheesecake home with her.

I'm emotionally exhausted and missing Gabe so I take the opportunity to thank everyone for being here and retreat to the bathroom where I run a bubble bath and relax into the steamy foam with my phone.

GABE

Sitting alone on the balcony, I reflect on the interview I just watched, hoping Sophia sat through it okay.

A bottle of scotch sits on the table beside me, and I refill my glass. Taking another puff on my cigar, I think back to the last time I had one. The night I told Sophia I was moving to London.

Despite my current predicament, it's the best decision I ever made. My phone pings with a message beside me, and hope causes my heart rate to spike when I see it's Sophia.

Sophia: *Watched your interview. Thank you x*

I stare at the screen for a while, debating whether to respond. I don't want to push her to talk. Asking how she is would be an insensitive move. I tap out a response three times, deleting each one. Then I settle on short and honest.

Me: *I miss you x*

Immediately, dots begin dancing across the screen. They stop and start again a few moments later. Perhaps she's having the same issue of what to say on her end. It's a few minutes before a message bounces back.

Sophia: *I miss you too x*

Relief washes over me. There's still hope for us. Ten minutes and another scotch later, I'm still contemplating sending her another message.

Me: *When are you coming home?*

Deflated when the message status updates to *read* but there's no sign of a response in progress, I ask Alexa to play music and recline into the lounger. Just like last night, I'll spend it outside as far away from my empty bed as possible.

Two songs into Alexa's selected playlist, the phone pings with a new message, and I snatch it up in a flurry, desperate for good news.

Sophia: *I forgive you, but I'm not ready yet x*

She didn't say no. All I can do is be patient and wait.

And continue to have faith in our love and the relationship we have built.

Chapter 35

SOPHIA
Two Weeks Later

"I won't take no for an answer, Jarett." I hear Gabe growl at my brother from the bathroom. The morning sickness has turned into all-day sickness, and I feel like a constant wreck—bloated, knackered, and emotional.

"It's been two weeks. She asked for space, and I've given her two fucking weeks. This ends today. Either she comes home with me, or we're done."

I clean myself up, pop a mint in my mouth, and shuffle out to meet the man I've been trying to avoid.

"Well, you'll have to wait until she stops throwing up."

"The fuck! She's still sick?"

"I'm not sick, I'm pregnant."

Gabe chokes on a smile. "We're having a baby?"

He rushes to me and pulls me against him, wrapping me in his arms. I notice Kassidy and Jarett leave the room as the waterworks spring another leak.

Roman and Jarett have both been in contact with Gabe and settled their differences. They both believe he shouldn't be punished for the actions of his father, and I agree. While I've struggled to move past him keeping it a secret, regular therapy is helping.

"Does this mean it's good news?" I whisper-sob into his shoulder.

"It's a fucking surprise but one I've never been happier to hear."

"How long have you known?" he asks, pulling back from me.

Guilt washes over me as I tell him. "You let me fly to New York without knowing?"

"You flew to New York to disclose a secret to the world without telling me. And it was a secret I *should* have known before anyone."

He releases a sigh and takes my hands. "I know, sweetheart. I fucked up, and if I could do it all again, I'd have told you sooner."

Nodding, I wipe the tears from my eyes with the back of my hand.

"Were you going to tell me about the baby?" he asks seriously.

"Always. I just didn't know when. I'm still trying to process everything."

"Can you at least come home so we can process it together?"

Home.

The truth is, I'm not staying here because I haven't forgiven him. While I don't appreciate what he did, I understand. Not knowing how to approach the baby news is what's keeping me here. That and feeling so damn shitty every day, it's difficult to muster up the courage or motivation to do much at all.

"I'd like that."

Gabe pulls me in and kisses me hard. He teases my lips open with his tongue and devours my mouth. My hands slip around his neck, and I hold him to me, missing the feel of his body against mine and his kisses. Boy, does this guy know how to kiss.

"Mmm, I've missed you."

"Me, too," I whisper, not wanting to let him go.

"Hey, you two love birds, we're about to order some noodles. Would you both like to join us?"

"Actually, we were..."

I cut Gabe off for the love of food. "Noodles sound amazing. Yes, please."

Gabe laughs. "I guess we're staying for dinner, then."

"She's eating for two now, but it's been a struggle for her to keep anything down until dinner."

Kassidy smiles at us both before she disappears to place the order.

"Sorry, I'm starved. Can we go home after dinner?"

"I'm holding you to it."

"I know it's early in the reconciliation days," Jarett begins, and I roll my eyes as I fight with my chopsticks. "Are we still planning a wedding for September 8th next year?"

Gabe shoots him a look I'm not familiar with, and Kassidy giggles.

"What's going on?"

"I'm sorry, but if you keep the original date, you'll have a baby on your hip. I was imagining your designer wedding gown with one of those baby harnesses stuck to the back."

Narrowing my eyes at her, I scold her silently until we all crack up laughing.

"And you may not fit in the gown you'd like after the baby," Jarett adds, and Gabe cringes beside me.

"Ex. Cuse. Me!" I bite out, horrified at the idea of both gaining baby weight and never looking as hot as I do now, ever again. Glancing at Gabe, I grin. "You put them up to this, didn't you?"

He holds his hands up in defense, "Hell, no, I never mentioned anything about harnesses or your figure."

I consider both of those for a few minutes as we continue eating in silence.

"What if you're right? My body will never look this way again after spitting a watermelon out of my lime. And I already have an eye on the dress I want."

"You do?" All three of them answer at once.

"Gosh, why so surprised? You all know I love shopping."

Gabe covers my hand with his on the table. "You certainly do. It's just, you've never mentioned a dress before. In fact, you've never wanted to discuss any of the details about the wedding."

Before I respond, I roll my eyes, biting my lip. "That's because I used all my energy trying to fight the idea of this fake wedding. But I fell in love with you, and now I want to get married," I rub my hands over my still flat stomach, "... as soon as possible."

"As in next week?"

Glancing around, I see all eyes are watching me intently. "There's something going on, and I'm out of the loop," I say. "Why the sudden rush?"

"You literally just said *as soon as possible*," Kassidy reminds me, and Gabe grins hard, his eyes pleading for an answer.

My mind drifts momentarily to my parents.

Planning a wedding they will never be a part of is emotionally challenging. "We haven't even discussed a venue or guest list," I add nervously.

Gabe turns in his seat and pulls me around to face him. "Sweetheart, you can have whatever kind of wedding you like. Big, small, grand, simple, I don't give a fuck, so long as you marry me."

"Let me sleep on it."

Chapter 36

SOPHIA
Two Weeks Later

"Gabe, get out!" I squeal, hearing him approach the door to the guest room.

"Why, what are you hiding in there?"

Slamming the door in his face, I return to the closet. "Give me a minute, please."

He huffs like a child sent to the naughty corner as I continue to zip up the garment bag to secure my gorgeous silver-blue ombre vintage fifties gown.

This halter neck design with a cream Chantilly lace overlay was made for me. The skirt is full, and the bodice shows off my curvaceous chest and slim waist. With early signs of a baby bump, it fits a little tighter than it did when I first put it on, but I felt like my mother the moment I stepped into it weeks ago, and I can't think of anything more perfect for my special day.

Smiling wistfully, I close the door and step out into the hall, where I find Gabe leaning against the wall patiently. "Did you buy your dress?" he asks with his signature cheeky smirk that causes me to forget my damn name.

"Yes, and it's bad luck for you to see it before the ceremony, so this room…" I point to the guest room door I pulled shut behind me, "… is off limits to you."

Laughing, he agrees. "Does this mean we're good for a close friends and family wedding on the rooftop this Saturday?"

It's only two days away, but yes. "Oh, I'm so ready to become your wife."

He pounces with excitement, pushing me against the wall and kisses me deeply. "Always and forever." When he pulls away, my mind is a lust-induced fog. Damn these pregnancy hormones, my libido is super-charged, and I'm constantly consumed with desire for this man. I attempt to pull him back to me when he bends over and kisses my tummy.

"How's my baby boy doing?"

And just like that, my sexual cravings disappear.

"What's that look?"

"You know it's going to be a girl, right?"

He smiles widely. "Either way, I don't mind. Are you sure you don't want to find out?"

"You're never going to give up, are you?"

"Nope." He chuckles, whisking me off my feet and storming into our bedroom.

Gabe sets me on my feet, and with a strong sweep of his tongue across my lips, I open to him, my hands rapidly removing his clothes while he strips me naked. We're all hands and broken breaths. "Fucking love you," he moans, peppering kisses across my cheek to my ear. I stretch my neck to the side as he nibbles, caressing my skin with his lips all the way to my collarbone.

Once we're both naked, Gabe pushes me back onto the bed. I scurry upward, Gabe's dark, hungry eyes following every movement like a predator on the hunt. He climbs up the bed, his broad shoulders rippling as he prowls over me. Teasing my inner thighs with sweet kisses, I quiver beneath his affectionate touch. He draws a nipple into his mouth, sucking gently, aware of their tenderness.

But fuck, it feels so good. His thumb and finger twist the other puckered nipple until I'm squirming, clawing at his back, unable to get close enough to the man I'm about to marry. His presence is overwhelming in the best way.

"Gabe, I need you inside me." I gasp when he pops my nipple from his mouth and kisses the other. His lips trace a path to my throat as he centers his body over mine, the head of his cock tapping at my entrance.

"Fuck, Soph. Your pussy is so wet."

"Only for you, Gabe."

"I own you, Sophia."

"Always and forever."

Gabe enters me with ease, his long, thick cock my favorite intrusion. Moving together as one, the friction of his pelvis over my clit has me at a four out of five on the orgasm scale in a matter of seconds.

"Gabe," I whisper, grinding into him, chasing my bliss.

He knows I'm close. In one swift movement, he rolls to his back, pulling me with him.

I sit back and cup my breasts. Gabe's hands squeeze my thighs, holding me in place as I ride his cock. My head falls back, and he instantly demands my attention.

"Look at me while you fuck me, Sophia."

His mouth falls open when I rotate my hips, changing up the pace. Rocking back and forth, I pick up speed again and collapse over him. Gabe clutches me to his chest and pumps his hips harder until I'm shaking uncontrollably. "Kiss me, Gabe. Fuck me with your tongue while I come on your cock."

"Love your dirty mouth," he groans and kisses me deeply.

Seconds later, my moans morph with his groans. I sit back slightly to watch him come undone beneath me as my pussy clenches around him and pleasure bursts from my core.

Rolling to the side, I snuggle against him while we catch our breath. Gabe runs his hand through my hair, relaxing me, lulling me close to sleep.

"You absolutely certain sex won't hurt the baby?" Gabe whispers.

Silently I giggle, hiding my face in his neck. "Don't laugh, I'm serious." He chuckles.

"I wasn't laughing," I lie, chuckling out loud.

"Your silent giggles were shaking the bed." He rolls me over and pins my hands above my head.

His love for me burns in his eyes, and I know right then, I am the luckiest woman alive.

"I'm coming to the next appointment with you, just to be sure."

Laughing again, I agree. "I want you at all the appointments, Gabe."

"Good, because I'm going to be the most hands-on dad you've ever known."

"Even if we have a girl?"

"Yep." His face screws up. "Except for the diaper changes, they're all yours, regardless of the sex."

Flipping my eyes back at him, I accept this. "Fine."

"I'm going to miss you when you go back to work."

Technically, I'm still working, but I only go into the office for four to five hours during the day when

I'm feeling at my best. After the wedding, we're going to honeymoon in Greece for a week, and I'll return to work at the office full-time afterward.

"In six months, you'll have me back at home fulltime," I remind him.

"I'm counting down the days already." He moves to my side and rubs my stomach.

"Is it strange that I can't wait for your baby bump to grow?" He kisses my torso, goosebumps breaking out over my sensitive flesh. "You're going to be the most beautiful pregnant wife and a perfect mother, Sophia."

His affection makes me tear up. "What if you hate my body after it's all stretched out of shape?"

Sadly, I'm coming to terms with the fact my skin may stretch and scar, and my boobs will soon be hanging around my navel. At least that's what I make of all the mom-to-be forums I've been ferociously searching through online.

"You'll always be gorgeous to me, I promise."

Chapter 37

SOPHIA
The Wedding

Although my morning sickness has subsided a lot, it's the evenings when I feel the best. That's why we decided to get married on the rooftop in the evening with Central London lit up in the background.

Ben flew in yesterday from New York, the only person Gabe wanted to invite to the wedding. Roman, Jarett, Ben, and Gabe spent the night in a hotel downtown, a low-key bachelors evening, while all my favorite ladies spent the night at our place, fussing over me profusely.

This morning we converted half the suite into a beauty parlor—waxing, facials, and mani-pedis followed by hair and makeup for each of us.

Gabe insisted on a photographer to shoot the

entire day from breakfast on the balcony to the setup of the beauty stations, all the beauty madness and fun, getting into my dress, right through to after the wedding.

We agreed to keep it elegant but simple—canapes on the roof after the ceremony and group photos, followed by dancing and cutting of the cake.

The press requested exclusive access, but instead, we worked with the photographer on a contract to allow us to decide which of the photos we're happy for him to send to the papers. It works for him as it's extra money in his pocket.

"Sophia, the caterer is here!"

The cake matches my dress in color and style. It's a three-tier, cookies 'n cream cheesecake, decorated with baby blue floral arrangements and edible gold balls. It's a fifties chic vintage design that, given the number of guests, only needed to be half the size. My hope is to freeze the remainder in individual servings for my midnight snacks throughout the pregnancy.

It's a fucking genius idea.

The caterers roll the cake into the kitchen on their delivery trolley and transport it to the counter. For ease, it will remain in the kitchen. We intend to return to the suite for the cake-cutting part of the evening. At which point, we hope to kick everyone out to have hot, dirty sex before we pack for our honeymoon in the morning.

"Holy shit, how amazing does it look?"

"Ladies!" one of the event planners, I think her name is Helen, requests our attention. "It's time to get you all into your dresses. The groom will be arriving in less than forty-five minutes."

I clasp my hands together. This is actually happening. "I'm getting fucking married today," I shout, making everyone laugh. The music volume increases as the beauticians clear out the remainder of their equipment.

"Don't you dare cry and wreck your makeup," Helen warns as she moves me toward the mirror.

"I'm pregnant," I wail. "I told them to use waterproof mascara and lots of setting spray!"

"Oh, sweetheart, there's no barrier for happy tears. Reel in those emotions until after the photos."

"Yes, ma'am." I chuckle at the middle-aged woman when she frowns at me.

"Call me Helen, please."

"Of course." I smile, unable to remove the stupid look from my face if I tried.

"You look absolutely gorgeous. This dress is perfectly you."

I run my palms over the front of the dress, admiring it in the full-length mirror from every angle. The skirt sits perfectly, accentuating my miniature baby bump which looks like a mild case of the bloats.

A knock on the door pulls me from my pose.

"Come in," Helen calls when I give her the nod. Kassidy, Maxine, Holly, Kelli, Jules, Karyn, and Bell burst into the room in fits of giggles. When they fix their eyes on me, silence descends on the room.

Smiling widely, I hold my arms out and pirouette, amazed I have such balance when I'm insanely giddy with happiness. Their applause brightens my cheeks, and one by one, they step forward and cover me in compliments.

I am positively glowing.

"Pregnant bride looks brilliant on you, Soph." We all laugh, and I remind them I'm missing some pieces.

"We've got you covered," Maxine smiles, running to the cabinet on the other side of the room.

"You all look so beautiful," I tell them. Seeing them all together in one room, I'm overcome with my love for the women in my life—strong, determined, graceful, and always have my back.

Max returns with a large shallow box I recognize as my mother's. "Something borrowed," she says, taking my mother's pearls in her hands. I fight the pending tears as she clasps the necklace at the back, and I thread the matching drop pearls through my ears.

Holly approaches with a small velvet pouch. Three generations. My grandmother's sapphire brooch she wore on her wedding day. So did my mother, and if Mom were still alive today, she'd insist I wear it too. "Something old and blue," she says, securing the brooch through the ribbon threaded through my up-styled hair.

"Something new," Kassidy adds, passing me a small gift bag. Inside is a gorgeous silver Chantilly lace wedding garter. "I'm so in love," I coo, blinking rapidly to avoid an overflow of tears.

I hold onto Kassidy's arm as I slide it over my heel and up my thigh.

"Sophia!" Roman yells. "Everyone is ready to go."

Maxine offers to let him know we're on our way up. I'm walking down the aisle alone today. We agreed on no bridesmaids or best man. The people we love will be with us, and those who can't be, don't deserve to be replaced.

So, if we can't have one, we forego the others. I expected it to be difficult, but it's the best decision, and I'm completely at ease with it now the day is here.

I wave goodbye to my favorite gals when Max returns. She's been tasked with walking me to the rooftop, where she'll then take a seat with the others. When the music commences, it's my cue to enter the area prepared for our special day.

And I can't wait to see what Gabe has done with the space.

Nerves dance wildly around my stomach as we carefully navigate the stairs to our private garden. The sun has gone down, and the city lights are glowing in the distance when I step onto the terrace. Max kisses my cheek and leaves me shaking in my stilettos.

Breathe, Sophia.

Just breathe.

As I remind myself how lucky I am, I marvel at the fairy lights lining the edge of the walls. Pendant lights hang from the overhead beams adding to the beauty. The music begins, and my breath hitches, but it stops a few seconds in. Kassidy races around the corner with my bouquet of white and baby blue roses and tosses them to me. "Sorry," she shrieks and dashes off again.

The music starts again, and I'm in awe as I round the corner. My eyes land first on Gabe in his royal blue suit, hair slicked back, and the deliciously cheeky grin I've come to love. His eyes are full of love and desire.

I want to run to him, but my legs are shaky, so I watch my step as I move through the scattered rose petals through the two rows of chairs on either side toward my groom.

My future husband.

The white wedding arch displays a matching bouquet of flowers on each corner, the sheets blowing peacefully in the autumn night breeze. I risk a glance at Roman and Jarett in the front row as I pass by, their smiles as wide as my own and filled with happiness.

Gabe extends his hand to welcome me to the official spot where we promise each other forever and always. "You look absolutely stunning, sweetheart." I curtesy and offer him a radiant smile, too choked up at the sight of this sexy hunk of man to speak.

We agreed not to exchange vows because I'm not the least bit traditional. Plus, with all these baby hormones kicking around my body, I'll be a blubbering mess, and we can't have a tear-stained face for the photos we'll share for the rest of our lives.

The marriage officiant acknowledges me with a nod when I stop fidgeting, and the ceremony begins.

Chapter 38

SOPHIA

"I now pronounce you, husband and wife. You may kiss the bride."

We did it. I'm married as fuck.

Gabe kisses me until I'm breathless and aroused. "Forever and always, I love you, Gabe."

Our friends applaud and cheer and as we walk toward them, hand in hand. My heart melts as they each release a Chinese lantern into the air with their personalized well wishes for our marriage attached.

I'm in awe at the setting, the way my man, my *husband,* pulled all of this together with the help of our incredible friends and family in two short days.

Waiters serve us canapes and bubbles, grape juice for me, on the rooftop while music plays out over the jukebox Gabe had delivered today. He bought it, of course, rather than renting one. In our forever home, with my forever man, I imagine many more gatherings on this rooftop, and I couldn't be fucking happier.

Gabe takes my hand when "Perfect" by Ed Sheeran comes on, the song we chose as *ours* for this special day. We glide around the makeshift dance floor in the middle of the gardens, two souls now one. When the song finishes, the others join us, and the real party begins.

A few hours later, I'm struggling to keep my eyes open, and Gabe suggests we go downstairs to cut the cake. My tummy grumbles with a *hell yes* and we herd like cattle into our suite.

"Don't forget to throw the bouquet, Soph," Kassidy whispers before she joins the others on the opposite side of the table. Now that's one tradition I *will* follow because I want to see which one of my single friends will be next in line to tie the knot. Happily married for only a few hours, I want this day for all my favorite people.

As we slice through the cake, a chorus erupts. *"Always and forever."*

It couldn't be more perfect. Gabe smears cheesecake over my bottom lip for the cameras and licks it off with his skillful tongue. My childish brothers groan and shout, "Get a room," making me laugh into our kiss.

We leave the catering team to serve the cake and

move into the living area where we toast yet again to our new life together. "To my billionaire fling, who wouldn't take no for an answer, thank you." I smile, a tear in my eye as I stare into the dreamy chocolate eyes that set my world on fire a little over a year ago. "I promise to be the best wife and mother to our child any man could ever hope for."

He sweeps me off my feet, leans me over, and kisses the ever-loving shit out of me again. I'm panting when he sets my feet back on the floor, suddenly eager for our guests to leave, so I can have my wicked way with my husband.

"One last thing before we eat the cake and kick you all out." I grin, turning with my back to everyone. "Men, move aside." They scurry like ants up the drainpipe in the heavy rains, and I toss the bouquet over my head, turning as Maxine fumbles and catches it. We can't help but laugh at the excitement on her face, and everybody in the room claps.

Except Roman.

His eyes are dark and piercing as he watches Maxine. Her gaze is equally as focused on him.

I make a mental note to ask some serious questions of those two when we return from Greece.

When it's time to throw the garter, it's Roman who claims it and his stormy gaze is cast over Maxine once again.

There is definitely something going on between those two. More than usual.

GABE

With all our guests finally out the door, it's time to consummate our marriage. Picking Sophia up, I carry her across the threshold of our bedroom door. I strip naked and run a shower for the both of us while she removes her jewelry so I can help her out of her dress.

As it slips from her shoulders to the floor, I admire her slender figure and imagine my beautiful wife as her belly grows. The idea of her carrying my child is the biggest turn-on.

Kneeling at her feet once her breasts are free, I take Sophia's thong in my teeth, slowly dragging it down, purposely nipping at the tender skin behind her knee. Peppering kisses over her foot as I remove it fully, her arousal floods my senses and makes my cock throb.

"Let's shower."

Sophia chuckles as I pick her up and carry her to the shower. "I'm perfectly capable of walking, you know."

"Conserving your energy for the important part of the evening, sweetheart."

We spend a few minutes lathering each other up, leaving no skin untouched. I commit every curve and freckle to memory. "I have the most beautiful wife."

"Oh yeah?" she says, taking my cock in her hand.

Pulling us both beneath the steaming flow of water, I devour her mouth. Our tongues dance as our hands explore, and our moans grow louder. *Needier.*

"How do you feel about shower sex to consummate this marriage?" I growl as I ravage her neck with kisses, pushing her against the wall. Waiting isn't an option.

"Hurry up and fuck me already," she groans, parting her legs for me and gripping my shoulders. I laugh at her eagerness and don't waste another minute.

Instantly, I lift her, and drive my cock into her pussy. Wrapping her legs around my hips, she grinds over my cock, matching my every move. Her hands rip at the back of my hair, her heels dig into my ass, and I pump harder, giving everything I have to be as close to this woman, my wife, as I possibly can.

"Feels so good..."

"Nothing better, sweetheart," I growl, biting her neck.

Her body begins to quiver in my hold, and her pussy clenches tighter around me. My balls are slapping and the steam bellows around us, my mind is lost to the pleasure she evokes from me "Come with me, sweetheart."

My fingers sink deeper into her outer thighs as I slam her down harder over my cock as I erupt inside her. At the same time, she cries out, her eyes roll back in her head, and my name falls from her lips.

The sweetest fucking sound I've ever heard.

"So beautiful," I whisper. "And forever mine."

Once we've recovered from our post-orgasmic bliss and towel off, I deliver my gorgeous bride to our bed and make sweet love to her again and again. Until night turns to day and our married life truly begins.

EPILOGUE

SOPHIA
Six Months Later

"Sit down and put your feet up, sweetheart."

Ugh. My last day at the office couldn't come quick enough. I'm exhausted, blown up like a balloon at the fair, and my feet are double the size when I can see them.

I'm a hot fucking mess and so ready to have this baby.

"How are you feeling about taking time off now you're here?" Gabe asks. I've been struggling with taking time off, leaving my first child in the hands of others while I concentrate on motherhood and enjoy time with our baby.

"I'm okay, I think. The guilt will ease once I'm holding our bub in my hands, I'm sure. And I'm never far away, I can do most things from home and pop into the office with the baby whenever I feel the need."

"Exactly, and I'll be here, Sophia. Between us, she'll be the luckiest little girl alive."

Yeah, Gabe won the battle over finding out the sex early. I gave in once we started discussing the nursery décor.

"Ten days, Gabe. What if I can't last until then?" I groan as my little girl stretches out and kicks me beneath the rib cage. "You little bugger," I curse, repositioning myself so I can breathe.

"Then I guess we'll be seeing our baby sooner which we're absolutely, one hundred percent prepared for."

I shake my head, "No, I want her out now because I'm worried I won't survive another ten days."

Gabe laughs at me, "Sweetheart, you're perfectly capable." He rubs my belly, and I realize that my stomach will be a flabby mess within a few weeks, and I'm going to miss the constant attention.

"Why don't you take a shower and freshen up while I prepare dinner?"

Internally, I groan at the mention of having to move, but if I sit here for too long, I won't be able to get up. Gabe offers me a hand as I roll to my side and shuffle off the sofa. Feeling sorry for myself, I waddle to our room, stopping by the nursery on my way.

It's my favorite room in the suite—lots of natural light, the crib covered in designer baby bedding and pillows, and a mix of sweet pastel colors.

The chest of drawers is filled with the cutest baby outfits ranging from newborn to six months to get us through the changing seasons, and the closet is overflowing with toys and keepsakes that won't see the light of day for at least a few months. The changing station is fully stocked and loaded with lotions, powders, nappies, and every self-care item any book I read ever mentioned.

We're definitely prepared to bring our girl home.

My favorite part of the room is the lullaby night light and the nursing chair with a footrest. Most nights, when I can't sleep, I find myself in here listening to the music, watching the twinkling stars on the ceiling, and imagining the books I'll be reading to her over the years to come.

Gabe had a built-in bookshelf designed to hold all the books I kept from when we were young. Every week, I've added to the collection. If I don't settle down, our baby girl will need a library room of her own before her first birthday.

The shower holds me hostage longer than intended, the hot water soothing my aches and pains. Instead of joining Gabe in the kitchen, where he's preparing my favorite home-cooked meatballs, I relax into the bed.

On the verge of dozing off, I clutch at my bump

as it spasms, and the dull pain in my hips increases. Sleep is a necessary evil. I can't function without it, my body begs me to sleep twenty-four-seven, but I can't sit or lay down for long without discomfort forcing me to move.

How have women been doing this for centuries? I have every kind of pillow there is—breastfeeding pillows, waist pillows, reading pillows—to help alleviate my discomfort, and still, I can't sleep.

"Sweetheart," Gabe says from the doorway. "Dinner is served."

"Be right there, thank you."

The pressure on my pelvis tonight is the worst it's been, and while I'm starving, I fear there's nowhere to fit the large number of meatballs I plan to devour.

I startle awake, pressure building in my stomach. The dull pain from earlier is back with a vengeance. As I roll out of bed with difficulty, I groan and check the time. It's three in the morning. When I try to stand, I'm forced back to the edge of the bed as a ripple of pain shoots across my pelvis. Thankfully, it passes relatively quickly.

I make it to the bathroom and flick the light on.

"Gabe," I shriek as a gush of fluid covers my feet and the floor. "Either I just peed myself or my water broke." Panic sets in. It's been months since I've had a panic attack, and my therapist has given me many ways to deal with them, none of which I can remember as I stand in the doorway of our bathroom.

"It's okay, sweetheart," Gabe whispers, sopping up the mess with a towel. "Are you in pain?" His look of horror mirrors my own.

"Only the dull pain I had last... argh." I double over as the shooting pain returns.

"I take that as a yes. I'm calling the doctor."

With the floor now dry, I fix myself up, and Gabe orders me to wait to shower until he returns.

The constant pain increases and the tightening across my abdomen becomes more regular. I've experienced a few Braxton Hicks over the past month but nothing like this. "Let's get you showered and changed, then we're off to the hospital, sweetheart. Doc said to monitor the time between the contractions. I need to call him when we get on the road."

My shower is brief, my overnight bag has been prepared for weeks, and we're out the door in less than fifteen minutes. Viktor meets us out front with a look of concern when I stop halfway to the car in pain. "Gabe, they're coming closer together."

We're only fifteen minutes from the hospital at this time of the morning, but it feels like hours. "They're about twenty seconds apart now. Okay, we will. Thanks, Doc." Gabe ends the call and wraps his arm around me. His comfort does little to make me relax.

"Can you call Jarett and Roman, please?"

Gabe dials Jarett first and hits the speaker button. "J, it's time," I say when he answers in a less than happy manner. "What time?" he grumbles. Rolling my eyes, I hear Kassidy in the background. "Give me the phone, you plonker."

"Sophia, is the baby coming?"

Thank God Jarett has a woman in his life. "On our way to the hospital now."

"We'll meet you there. Good luck. We love you."

As I breathe through the next contraction like I've just run a marathon, Gabe calls Roman.

"Gabe?" he answers, a little more alert than Jarett was.

"Roman, we're on our way to the hospital. Today's the day, this baby is coming."

It sounds like he's getting out of bed. "We'll be right there, Soph."

"Thank you, can you call Max for me? We're about to pull up."

"I'm here, sweetie. See you soon."

Maxine?

"Aahh," I groan, unsure if it's the contraction or

hearing Maxine's voice that surprises me more.

Gabe is about to end the call when I screech, "Wait."

When the pain passes, I take the phone from him. "Max, it's three-thirty in the morning. Are you *sleeping* with my brother... again?"

Max laughs, but it's Roman who answers with a grunt. "You're about to have a baby, Soph. How about you concentrate on that for now?"

My mouth falls open, annoyed I'm not going to get any gossip in my time of need. "Great advice. We'll see you both soon." Gabe ends the call and places a finger over my lips as I'm about to give him a piece of my mind.

"Ugh." *Men.*

Exactly thirty-eight minutes after I'm wheeled through the hospital doors, I'm lovingly staring at our baby girl in my arms. Gabe sits with us on the edge of the bed, wrapping us both in his love.

"You did great, sweetheart." He kisses my head and strokes our little princess.

Tears of joy stream down my face. I can't stop staring at our red-faced bundle of joy.

"Your family is asking if they can see you," the nurse says.

Grinning from ear to ear, no longer concerned with how exhausted I am, I tell her to let them in.

Baby balloons and flowers are paraded into our room by our over-the-top family who dote on our little bundle of joy, offering Gabe and me all the praise.

"Does my cute little niece have a name yet?" Roman asks, deliriously excited about his new uncle status.

"She does. Sienna Gabrielle Lugreno." My mother's middle name and the female version of Gabe's birth name. I pass our little bundle of joy to her daddy and reposition myself, making sure all my bits are covered.

"She's beautiful, guys," Kassidy swoons.

"Look out, J. Kassidy here is getting all clucky."

"So what if I am," she defends with a cheery grin.

"Well..." Jarett says, wrapping his arms around her, "... you do only have a month until your contract is up, so..."

"What?" Kassidy laughs. "You want to knock me up so I can stay?"

Roman pipes up, "I think legally, you'd be required to marry her so she can get a visa." There's always one in the room obsessed with legalities.

I glance across at Gabe, who finally lifts his eyes away from the baby. "Or, you could take my offer of a full-time position and stay indefinitely, visa and all the legalities taken care of?"

"Oh my God, Gabe, are you serious?" Kassidy bounces and flings herself into Jarett's arms.

"Fuck yes." Jarett grins, shaking Gabe's hand.

"Yes, yes, yes, I accept." Kassidy kisses Gabe and

plays with Sienna's little fingers while cooing in a baby voice.

"Thank you," I mouth to Gabe when his eyes meet mine. This day couldn't possibly get any better.

Maxine shoves Roman, and sheepishly, he adds, "While we're all in the celebrating mood, Maxine and I have something to share too."

My chest beats rapidly with the excitement of what I assume is coming.

"Months ago, when I told you the news about me taking on the chef position at Maximum, I left out the most important and exciting part of the announcement." He glances at Maxine who's outrageously glowing.

"What I didn't tell you is Maxine and I are dating."

"I knew it. How could you hide this from us?" I whisper-yell. When I asked them both what was going on when we returned from our honeymoon, they denied everything.

"From all of us?" Jarett adds. "How long have you two been *dating*?"

"Since just after Sophia's birthday," Max announces, taking Roman's hand.

I cry, overwhelmed with happiness. "When you know, you know," I say, remembering the conversation we had the day I found out I was pregnant.

This is the longest they have ever stayed together. Between the on-again, off-again attempts at a relationship, there's been plenty of nights over the years, but this makes my heart so happy.

"And you caught the bouquet," I sob. Gabe is laughing at my emotional outburst.

"Yeah, we're hoping to hold off until little Sienna is walking." Max smiles. "We'd like her to be our flower girl."

"Aww, you two, I love you so much. And yes, Sienna will make the perfect flower girl.

Next in the Series:

My Forever Fling: Roman and Maxine's Story (British Billionaires Book 3)

Maci Dillon

Other Series by Maci Dillon

British Billionaires

Unrequited Love

Twice the Fun

Beachmont Players

And more…

Subscribe to the Minx Diaries
and receive a FREE eBook.
https://macidillonauthor.com/subscribe

Join Maci Dillon's Reader Group
https://facebook.com/groups/macidillonminxes

ACKNOWLEDGMENTS

Wow, what a journey it has been! There are so many people I would like to thank by name, and I trust you each know who you are.

Bossman and my kids, you are my life, and your support means the world to me. Thank you. xx

To Sara, my PA, you help to make all of this possible, keeping me on track while I'm head down in the writing cave. Thank you. xx

Minxes, you're my greatest supporters in the book world, and this means so much to me. I can never thank you enough for your friendship, encouragement, and everything you do to share my words with more readers. You all rock. xx

My amazing editing team, thank you! Kaylene,

Nicki, and Chantell, you're the best! xx

KE Osborn, huge shout out for the cocktail title graphics for this series – I freaking love your work! xx

Sarah at Opium House, your cover designs are on point. I love working with you, and thank you for bringing my visions to life. xx

A huge thank you to Em and Ellen for your notes, input, and suggestions on this book. Without you, I'd be starting over for the fourth time. LOL xx

To every member of my ARC Tribe, bloggers, book influencers, readers, and reviewers, your support motivates and encourages me always. Thank you for loving Gabe and Sophia and for sharing them far and wide. xx

Best wishes,
Maci Dillon

ABOUT THE Author

Maci Dillon is a self-confessed lover of margaritas who has recently experienced her very own second chance at true romance.

Maci is a daydreamer and true minx at heart who loves to read and write steamy romance filled with love, lust, angst, and humor. Her favorite tropes to write are second chances, forbidden romance, enemies to lovers, menage, reverse harem, hate sex, drunken hookups, playboys, and billionaires. She also enjoys writing raunchy short stories within these tropes.

Her heroines are strong, experienced, foul-mouthed, and feisty with loads of sass and wit. Her men are deliciously hot, dominant, often arrogant, and entitled smart-asses. You will experience all the feels across Maci's books.

You will often find Maci in her PJs writing and watching Netflix. She is an expert procrastinator, a superior planner, except with her writing, and loves a social drink and barbecue with friends and family.

Maci lives in Brisbane, Australia, and is a mother of three teenagers and a Maltese Shih Tzu.

Visit my Website!
https://macidillonauthor.com/

Printed in Great Britain
by Amazon

62230926R00167